EAST SIDE OR DIE
(CHRONICLES)

EAST SIDE OR DIE
(CHRONICLES)

By Christopher Trotter

Self-Published with help from
MIDNIGHT EXPRESS BOOKS

EAST SIDE OR DIE (CHRONICLES)

Self-Published with help from
MIDNIGHT EXPRESS BOOKS
POBox 69
Berryville AR 72616
(870) 210-3772
MEBooks1@yahoo.com

EAST SIDE OR DIE (CHRONICLES)

By Christopher Trotter

Dedicated to all the children who lost their lives to Chicago's violence. Saving our children starts with you!

More dedications go out to my three sons, the greater images of me.

In loving memory of my cousin Brandy Trotter from Sept.20, 1973 to Sept.20, 2011. May your spirit live on shorty!

Shout Outs

Shout Outs goes first to the Creator, The most high Yahweh. Shout Outs to my three sons, the recreated greater images of me. The World is yours! We in it and we leaving our mark in it. I'm proud of ya'll and I salute ya'll! Shout Outs to all those who continued to love and support me even when I was a menace in the ethers of Chicago's mayhem. That's my Dad, Mom, Grandma, and Aunties. I woke up and now I can see thanks to you all not giving up on me. Also Big Chris love the kids, love to my Niece and Nephews. Smile I see ya'll! Shout Outs to my real guys, my Fam. names need not be said.

To those I grinded with, struggled and hustled with, went out hunted and ate with. Who stood firmly pivoted back to back in the mist of fire with, never running but fighting to the end with me. Who when I was in distress, aided and assisted me especially when I was incarcerated. Who woke up with me. The wool is no longer pulled over our eyes we see the light. We coming out from the dark, from struggling to survive, fighting, and grinding under the moon light. Shout Outs to all the ladies who I share experiences in life with. Smile baby ya'll know who ya'll is. Shout Outs to all my men, those out there in it, about that life. Yeah I know these new jacks not doing it how we was. We was in it for real, they playing. Our gains were great just like our pains. Now it takes us to help fix what we broke. Let's try to clean up some of the mess we shitted out so our children's children will not continue to play and step in it.

Shout Outs remain nameless for street reasons but it need not be said because you all know who you are. Much Love!

East Side or Die

PROLOGUE

The following events took place sometime between 2005 & 2011

During the wee hours of a rainy Chicago night, a pair of bloodshot eyes locked onto an all white Escalade truck as its rims glistened in the moon light, spinning, then coming to a sudden stop on 88th and Saginaw. It parked directly in front of Sheila's house. The soul behind those blood shot eyes asked the only soul on the gangway with him, "What kind of rims do that hoe ass nigga Little 'O' got?"

His accomplice replied, "Some six's."

The soul behind those blood shot eyes then whispered, "This nigga just pulled up in front of that dick sucking rat bitch Sheila's house." Suddenly the only thing revealed in the mist of the night was the white from his accomplice eyes widening and teeth from a grin...

Meanwhile in the back of the Escalade, Tom-Tom pulled his dick out of Sheila's mouth and told her, "Go ahead and knock fam down, I got to take a piss." He emerged from the truck heading toward the side of Sheila's house.

As Sheila jumped up front, Little 'O' grabbed her head to shove his dick down her throat. She gagged, choked, and instantly gained control before moaning. Little 'O' bobbed her head with one hand and rubbed her fat ass with the other as he just couldn't resist telling her, "Bitch, bend over I gotta hit this."

While her big round booty made a clapping noise smacking against his body, with her face pressed against the passenger window, she frantically reached back tapping him whispering, "Little 'O', Little 'O'." He replied, "Yeah, I'm hitting it ain't I?"

She responded, "No fool look!"

As he looked up, they both observed Tom-Tom running towards them. They heard a gunshot, and witnessed him take a head shot that shattered the windows, leaving blood from his forehead splattered on Sheila's face, as she fell to the floor screaming.

Little 'O', moving faster than a jackrabbit, tried to jump behind the wheel but his face couldn't escape the ongoing load of bullets the other soul with blood shot eyes released.

He ran up to the driver's side of the truck to finish the job, leaving the remainder of Little 'O's face pressed against the horn.

Hours later, reporter Alicine Payne from W.G.N News reported, "Two men found dead and one woman is hospitalized from a shooting last night on Chicago's far eastside, the 88th block of Saginaw near Bowen High school. One man was found shot to death on the sidewalk, the other found naked, shot to death in an S.U.V, with a woman suffering from shattered glass cuts. Motive and suspects still unknown at this time."

Yeah, Sheila's a real certified slut bitch who got a bomb on the head. She'll suck a camel through a sewing needle hole. She loves a face load of cum but got a load of blood this time. These two niggas lost their heads getting some head. What caused it all? Just walk with me, I'ma take you back a little bit with a series of events starting from the beginning, but right now I know you asking, "Who the fuck am I?" From this point on, I'm gonna be the one narrating this shit. However, for the record, I'm the spirit of err.... A.K.A Lucifer. I'm welcoming you into my kingdom Hades/ Hell, known to you as the Eastside of Chicago. They say State to da Lake, yet it go far deeper than life.

The farther East you go, you enter different levels of Hades. Let me take you there. Give me your soul and allow your spirit to walk where we've walked, see what we've seen, feel what we've felt, smell what we've smelled, and think what we've thought. My motto is Hades... I mean East Side or Die Chronicles bitch, as I roam to and from the 79th to the 9-Tray, maneuvering throughout 87th to banging in the B's, defining terror in Terror Town, to enlightening my spirit in gangsta shit with my J.M.G's, then roaming the Jeffery Manor maze, a gangstas paradise, to before leaving hovering over the Back. From grinding with the grinders in Cercon City, to South C., where they make their rivals fight for survival. From Commercial to Bush, I'm crowned king at making brains gush. On Saginaw, 67th, 71st, Avenue A, B, C, and beyond, you'll see me. But where I be, Houston and Buffalo visiting those who imitate me, cause this a be the last time you bitches will ever witness a true mutha-fuckin' bad guy like me A.K.A Lucifer G. I'm praised as a gangsters gangster, a killers killer, a hustlers hustler, a kings king, and a pimps pimp, so when you're in the presence of I, continue to get high, throw your hoods up in the sky, and scream East-Side or Die!

CHAPTER ONE

During the past decade Chicago Known as Chi Town, like a heavy weight boxer, fighting for the title belt has had its share of being crowned as the murder capital. Now due to an extreme number of school kids losing their lives in these title fights, some community activist along with different religious leaders decided to-go out into their communities for action.

They asked questions, made suggestions, and ministered for ending Chicago's violence.

A Saturday Afternoon

As Muhad Shabazz in his Buick Lacrosse drove eastbound on 95th passing State Street, his wife Shafina said, "I don't like the feeling I've been feeling since we crossed State Street. The more viaducts we go under, the more the people seem possessed." She stated this while staring out the window observing her surroundings.

They pulled up, parked, and approached a crowd Harun Muhammad was speaking to in the parking lot of the Mosque on 89th Stony Island. Muhad saw a young man in his early twenties and greeted him with, "As-Salaam-Aleichem.

The young man looked at him with a strange face and said, "White women and pork chops to you too, my nigga."

Muhad's peaceful face instantly turned to a boiling rage as Harun interrupted with, "Muhad... come join us Akh."

As another gathering took place outside on 75th Street by a Hebrew Temple, a young dark skinned man with a Sox baseball cap on yells from out the crowd, "How ya'll gone tell us to stop the violence, return to God, and about our people, when ya'll think ya'll some black Hebrews and black Jews. In that case, I'ma black clan member and the K.K.K is black."

Some young people within the crowd burst out laughing.

At the same time while this was taking place on 84th and South Chicago, Rev. Jackson was telling a crowd, "When facing confrontation, we must let Jesus have the victory and turn the other cheek."

A young man from the crowd wearing a white-T-shirt yelled out, "So if I kick Jesus in one ass cheek, do you actually think he gonna turn and let me kick him in the other one?"

The Rev responded, "Blasphemers will burn for eternity in Hell."

Two youths from the crowd threw raw eggs at the preacher, leaving egg yolk running from off his face.

The Rev. stated to the crowd, "What would Jesus do?"

The young man in the white T-shirt yelled, "Tell your Jesus to turn that egg yolk running down your face into a multitude of scrambled eggs so you can feed the crowd with it."

Half the crowd started laughing until gunshots rang out from across the street causing the crowd to scatter in a frantic attempt to gain cover.

An hour earlier

Kareem, Teno, and Big Face entered City Sports shoe store on 91st and Commercial and headed towards the shoe racks. Kareem noticed the store full of haunty eyes that had faces full of mean mugs staring at Big Face.

Big Face seem not to be paying any attention as he walked in wearing a blue Houston Astro's baseball cap broke off to the right side. He carried in his right hand a bag that read Rainbow on the side with clothes in it for his daughter.

Kareem told him, "You got eyes on you, fam."

He responded, "I been peeped that, but fuck them rock ass niggas, they ain't on shit!"

One of them then said, "Donut-ass niggas get their ears stomped together around here!"

Big Face dropped his bag and yelled, "What you bitches wanta do then?"

Teno, who was wearing a Bulls basketball cap slightly turned to the left side, approached the men and said, "Aye, Mid, calm down, they with me. Let me rotate with ya'll for a minute." Then, he went to the back of the store to talk with the guys.

Minutes later one of them loudly stated, "This the multitude right here, you ain't one of the Mids if you on that."

One of the guys hit Teno in the face causing him to fall and knock over a clothing rack.

As Big Face witnessed Teno take the hit, he reached into his pants to grab the handle of a rubber-grip, chrome 38, but hesitated pulling it out when he heard guns cocking.

Teno got up and said, "I'm O.K. It's cool... that's what the Mids on, huh?"

They recognized they were outnumbered and outgunned, so they calmly walked out the store with the crowd of Mids following fifteen feet behind.

A male spectator coming out a store next witnessed two shots fired from the crowd, Big Face hitting the ground with his Rainbow bag sliding two feet away, Kareem and Teno running towards the alley, then Big Face jumping up busting two shots back before hitting the alley with the crowd chasing behind.

The spectator picked up the rainbow bag and disappeared.

This was a case of being at the wrong place at the wrong time, because just days prior, a member of the Pyramids, known as the Mids for short, got changed. (A term used for murdered.) He was allegedly gunned down by a member of the Goblin mob gang from South Chicago, so the Mids were thirsty for vengeance in honor of their falling soldier.

Now as the crowd of Mids hit the alley, they decided to split up, each one lusting to get the badge-for striking down their prey.

Meanwhile, in the alley following behind Kareem and Teno, Big Face finally made it to the top of the barb-wired fence just as his gun fell out through his pants leg. Quickly he jumped down to retrieve it. He landed a few feet away only to find one of his hunters, Big Moe, running up aiming. He also noticed a man behind Big Moe with gun in hand, who shot him in the shoulder causing him to drop his gun and take off running.

The man said to Big Face as he held a Rainbow bag up in one hand, "Aye, nigga... you dropped my niece shit!"

Big Face was surprised to see his baby momma's brother, Fats, but postponed the family reunion by grabbing his gun and going after Big Moe, causing the hunted to now be the hunter.

As Big Face gained on his tail, all you heard was the panting from their breaths and the wind cutting across their faces while fences rattled from being jumped over in the pursuit. As they ran past a garage through the side cut-a-way of a house to its front yard, Big Face began to let his 38 cannon explode until he saw a church, end the Violence Rally across the street with its crowd frantically scattering from his shots. While his prey escaped in the crowd, he retreated, disappearing into the cut.

A little later

A deep fog of smoke filled a dark room, glowing in its darkness was the red flame from a blunt being passed around.

While Big Face watched Fats grab the blunt from out his dirty finger tips he said, "Aye, that shit you did today... that's how we hold each other down. I love you nigga. I'll go against the grain for you,

5

baby... we family." He looked around into all their eyes and continued, "On everything I'll kill and die with ya'll, this family here, ya'll hear me? We gone make it official. From this point on, we gonna be the fucking East-Side- Brothers... Aiiight! Together we stand; together we fall; as we kill em all."

Teno interrupted, "If we gone be doing all that, I hope we standing and falling on money while we kill em' all."

Big Face was six feet, 185 pounds and twenty years old. He's a light complexion black male, with long hair to his shoulders. Now after Teno's remark, he shook his head up and down with a big grin on his face as he stared at Teno for a moment, realizing that all organizations must have a financial base, which he was now determined to firmly establish.

He deeply inhaled on the blunt that was planted between his lips, reached for and slammed his 38 revolver on the table, and cut his knuckles with a razor blade they used to slice the blunt with. Then he poured Gin on his bleeding fist, set it ablaze, held his blazing clinched bleeding fist in the air, and rapidly made vows proclaiming, "We the East-Side-Brothers until death and beyond. Together we stand, fall, and kill em' all, first for each other second for wealth. It's E.S.B or Die!" He put the flame out, puffed a few more times and passed the blunt to Kareem who was now to do the same.

These rituals and vows was the beginning of a monstrous brotherhood mob on Chicago's east side that would never be forgotten.

Kareem

Kareem then took a few puffs off the blunt, slammed his nine millimeter gun on the table and followed through with the rituals and vows. Kareem who is a six-foot, 165 pound, eighteen-year-old, light skinned, black male, with natural curly hair in an afro, lived in the Jeffery Manor on Big Face's block. He was the good school-boy type who had N.B.A dreams. Even though Big Face and Kareem worlds were different, they hung out a lot, inviting each other into the others world and mixing them. Kareem showed Big Face a world he didn't think existed; a world of sanity. Big Face showed Kareem a world of the street insanity and how to let the spirit of mayhem enter your soul.

Kareem looked up to him as his big brother. He did whatever he said and wished he could possess the spirit Big Face had to be like him, while Big Face wished he possessed the skills Kareem had. Kareem had a nasty jump shot and played basketball all day at the park with the older guys breaking their ankles like the most valuable player of the N.B.A. If Kareem wasn't at school or on the court he was with Big Face witnessing gangster shit first hand or being taught gangster shit with hands on experience. Big Face embraced him as his little brother. He made sure he went to school, did his homework, and stay out of trouble. Big Face kept money in his pockets, and even fought his fights. Even though Big Face kept him with him on gangster shit, he always tried to keep his little brothers hands clean. He believed he was looking out for him by keeping him safe and out of trouble so he could make it to the N.B.A.

Kareem was in the (J.M.G) Jeffery Manor Goblin gang like Big Face but Big Face wouldn't let him gangbang or break his hat off to represent. Kareem's wicked jump shot brought him full scholarships from everywhere, yet he didn't want to leave Big Face so he never told him about all the offers. He later accepted an offer to attend (N.I.U) Northern Illinois University.

Once Kareem finished doing the rituals and vows, he exhaled smoke from the blunt and passed it to Teno to do the same in this ceremony.

Teno

Teno next took a few hard hits off the blunt, slammed his 380 gun on the table and followed through with the ritual and vows. Teno's a five-foot, 157 pound, nineteen-year-old, dark complexion, black male, with waves in his hair.

Teno and Big Face knew each other since the big wheel days and were like cousins. His mother, Gloria, used to baby-sit Big Face when they used to live in the same apartment building on 75th and Essex. Big Face eventually moved, but they kept in touch like real cousins. As they grew older, Teno, who was affiliated with the Pyramid gang and originally from Terror Town, moved in with his second baby momma Shaunika on 87th and Manistee. However, he continued to small-time hustle out of his first baby momma's Lala's house on 85th and Escanaba. Even though Big Face was in his own world, they somehow found time to hook up on a regular to get into some bullshit. Teno, like Kareem, went to school and did well. He was more of the playboy type but Big Face made him bring the gangster out when they hooked up. Since childhood, Big Face and Teno had dreams of being Rappers but mainly big business men owning everything. They both loved the system of supply and demand, trading for wealth, and the power it held. Now they'll both trade the blood of prey for capital.

Teno completed the rituals and vows, puff, puffed, and passed the blunt for Fats to do the same.

Fats / Keshia

Fats, the last one to embrace the blunt, inhaled it through his mouth and nose, slammed his 45 magnum gun on the table, and proceeded with the rituals and vows. He is a six-foot, 247 pound, twenty-two-year-old, dark brown complexion, black male, with a bald head. Fats is Big Face's baby momma's brother.

His sister is a caramel complexion five star chick name Keshia who has a 34-26-45 frame, with a face like Elise Neal, titties like Malesa Ford, with hips and an ass like Deelishis. She is your good-girl type that all the guys, even the females try to come up on, yet she would diss them all.

Big Face was making an early morning drug run when he seen her going to work. She dissed him but he kept riding by showing off every morning until she finally gave in. Months went by with the closest he got to the pussy was having her Apple Bottom jeans button popped open, with her thick thighs spread across the seats of his black-cherry, old-school 1984 Monte Carlo that sat on 24" rims. As the Kenwood speakers bumped a Drake song called, "You the best I ever had," with the lyrics singing, she made me beg for it till she gave it up...his fingers played in the juices of her tight hairy pussy.

As she sucked on his lip, he stuck his tongue in her mouth and that was the day he smelled his fingers with the sweet scent of her pussy, licked it, and vowed to fuck her rubberless.

One day when Big Face was standing on her porch with her heart shaped ass cheeks in his hands while tongue kissing, some guys on the corner of 85th Street started shooting at each other so she let him in.

Once inside she got the Hennessey and Patron drinks out before going to change into something more comfortable. He popped a double stack ecstasy drug pill and put some in the drinks before shaking them up. Keshia then came out in a red-and-white Victoria Secret lingerie outfit. Big Face's dick instantly stood up as he quickly gave her the drinks.

She didn't smoke but he influenced her to inhale the blunt he pulled out. While sitting on the couch in the living room, the ecstasy pill started to take effect on Keshia. She then felt her panties being moved to the side and her pussy lips being opened as a tongue began to give her moist coochie extreme pleasure. She grabbed Big Face's head and let a moan out as she spread her legs wide open. He next cuffed her ass and pulled her to the floor until she sat on his face. Keshia snatched her bra off revealing long hard nipples as she twisted around in the sixty-nine position to grab his balls, spit on his dick, 'Tuh', and suck it, 'Gulp'.

After that, he couldn't help but tell her, "I love your ass already." Her ass wiggled in his face until she came and moaned with his dick in her mouth causing a great vibrating sensation.

The speakers in the living room sang a Jeremiah song, "I'm gone take the time to love your body, rub your body, kiss and hug your body," he picked her up off the floor, carried her into the bedroom and laid her on her back. He put her feet up on the wall, grabbed her ankles, spread her pussy lips, and began pounding away.

Her pussy made a 'gush' sound from being so wet. He sucked on her long nipples and began to nut in her as his left leg shook. Once finished, he fell to the bed on his back, but she sucked him back hard and rode him making her pussy muscles squeeze his dick until she let her juices run down his dick unto his balls.

Then he flipped her to the doggy style position, spread her humongous butt-cheeks with his thumbs, and while looking down to see her anus revealed, couldn't help but to spit down on it, 'Tuh'. He then shoved his erect dick in her hot pussy and his thumb in her ass.

As her ass shook and made a clapping noise, she tried to crawl away.

He pulled her back by her hair and continued bouncing off her big butt, 'clap, clap, clap. He pushed deep inside her, forcing her head to hit the headboard as she moaned loudly, "Oh shit, baby, you fucking the shit out of- me!" Once again his left leg shook as he nutted all in her before falling to sleep. He might have laid his pipe game down, but he was officially pussy-whipped plus her head game was immaculate.

When they finally woke up, it was as if they had been a couple for years. Nine months later their daughter Alivia was born.

Keshia brother, Fats, was in the Legion gang known as the L's for short, from the 'B's, known as Burnham Street. Fats and his older sister lived in a family, two flat, apartment building on 85th and Burnham. He was locked up in prison for a kidnap robbery while Big Face was fucking his sister, until two years after Alivia was born. One afternoon when Fats and the Legions was in the house, Big Face came walking in to have a room full of guns drawn on him while he upped his 44 magnum. As Fats and Big Face stood with guns drawn face to face reading each other's soul, Keshia, who Big Face left in the drive-way getting Alivia out the car, came in yelling, "Fats, that's Big Face, Alivia's father. Ya'll put them fucking guns down now!" Fats and Big

Face somehow clicked after that. Fats liked how Big Face held his composure under pressure, and Big Face liked how Fats kicked it. They both recognized they shared and possessed a common spirit. After Fats finished the rituals and vows, he ate the remainder of the burning blunt.

Narrator, Lucifer

Now that's gangsta. Imagine seeing a burning fist, dripping blood, being held in the air like some black power shit. That statue of Liberty bitch holding a torch ain't got shit on them. Come on! I know you ain't go for that bullshit? Do you really think some alcohol will burn on your fucking hand long enough to get third degree burns? Then you got this last nut case eating the burning blunt like he gangsta. But hey, the mere sight of all this shit was gangsta. It's funny how this little mall gangbanging incident triggered a bond that soon exploded into the E.S.B, Eastside Brothers Mob. But, continue to walk with me as I guide your eyes to see how this self crowned captain and his generals heinous death before dishonor acts stack paper and corpse up. Let's now explore from this animal instinct beast the E.S.B.

CHAPTER 2

Big Face knew that by him being the one to officially establish this fraternal East Side Brotherhood Mob, he had to also be the one to establish its financial base in order to be taken serious. After some deep meditation, he finally came up with someone who was the solution to their problem. He knew he just couldn't accept the answer no, so he aggressively put his plan into motion.

A flashy platinum color Range Rover parked in front of the basketball court on 98th and Yates, to have a major hustler name Kevo jump out and yell, "I got next!" Kevo was a local basketball star who everyone knew would make it to the N.B.A until he got shot up. His injuries from that shooting killed his hoop dreams but awoke him to a prosperous reality in narcotics. Even though Kevo was from 85th and Exchange, and affiliated with the Legions gang, he didn't do the gangbanging thing. By him being a local basketball star he was welcome into all hoods and knew all the guys who were deeply rooted in the streets. After he got robbed and shot up at a club on the west side, the Mexican mafia persuasively recruited him. They knew he was liked by all the major hustlers in town due to his hoop skills and could go into all hoods. Making Kevo a major connect would greatly open up their pipeline from Mexico to Chicago.

Kevo and Kareem used to battle each other on the basketball court and was both known as the local future N.B.A stars. Now as Kevo crossed over his opponent and ran up the court, Big Face jumped inside his Range Rover as Kareem sat on the hood, causing his alarm to go off, and taking his attention off the court to them. Once they managed to get Kevo in the truck and to ride off, Big Face said, "Dig Kevo… we gone keep it one hundred and not play no games with each other. We hungry and we trying to eat. You got what we want. If you feed us, we can all get fat and fart. We ain't come empty handed, we just want that shit them terrorist got for the low-low and you being the man with it, we want you to be our man." Three hours later, blenders was blending dope and pots were boiling coke, while scales, razorblades, baking soda, cards, and baggies were being utilized to chef the final production of some potent narcotics.

Big Face and Fats, who was at the table mixing dope, decided to make a smoke and drink run so they went to the liquor store leaving Kareem and Teno at the table mixing dope. As they came out of Kenwood Liquors, Big Face said, "Let's see if the old lady at home." Fats, replied, "I'm trying to figure out how the fuck do that old Nigerian bitch and her son got the best shit in town but only a few know. That shit so fire that everybody and they momma suppose to be talking about that shit where they got traffic jams in front of that bitch."

Big Face responded, "That's exactly what they trying to avoid. That's why only a chosen few know. But I got to find out where they getting that shit from."

Fats banged on the side door and an old lady swung it open yelling in an Nigerian accent, "Fats ya betta stop banging on me door like ya lost ya fucking mind. I'm gonna break this cane across ya head. Big Face ya betta tell em'. Now baby ya come on in."

Once inside Fats said, "We need to halla at you and your son on some business."

When her son came in the room Big Face like he always does says to him, "Aye, man what's your name again?"

He answered in a strong Nigerian tone, "Kabiru."

Big Face said, "See, that's why I don't talk to you, cause I can't never understand shit you be saying."

When they all started laughing the front and side doors came crashing in with men wearing ski masks, flashing police badges, and guns, yelling, "Police, everybody on the fucking floor. You move, you get shot."

They raised their hands up in the air and laid on the floor as they was told.

One man with a Malsburg pump watched over all four of them laying on the living room floor, two other men searched the house, and one man stood guard outside the front door, and another outside the side door.

After a few minutes, one of the men searching the house came back and grabbed the old lady by her hair and pulled her up off the floor and drug her into the kitchen.

Big Face looked at Fats, then up at the shotgun pump and realized it was sawed off. He also noticed that they didn't search or cuff them. So now, he knew for a fact they weren't the police, but instead were men who came to steal and kill.

He looked at Kabiru who was scared to death lying in a puddle of his own piss, then back at Fats who was staring at the man with the pump. He slowly pulled his 45 magnum out. Big Face knew it was life or death so he snuck his hand under his shirt to unhook a W.W.J.D. (What Would Jesus Do) strap to give him quick and easy access to a tech nine, that was hooked to it.

As Fats shot the man holding the pump and another that came running in through the front door, Big Face flipped over onto his back to let the tech ride, chopping up one of the men in the house and another man running in through the side door. Then, Fats and Big Face jumped up off the floor busting shots, Big Face to the kitchen and Fats to the front of the house. Fats ran up squeezing his 45 to complete the hit just as the shotgun gave a final roar like thunder causing buckshots to strike his left arm.

While this was going on, Big Face ran in the kitchen to get the other dude. But when he got in the kitchen, he saw the other guy holding a gun to the old lady's head.

"I'll push this bitch shit back... you better let me get up out of here!" the guy told him.

Big Face responded, "I don't give a fuck, that bitch ain't my momma!"

The old lady fainted when she heard this and fell to the floor.

Then, Big Face let the tech ride, making the dude's body dance against the refrigerator before it fell to the floor.

When the old lady woke up as Fats and Kabiru ran into the kitchen, they yelled something in their own language to each other, then Kabiru ran off into another room. He came back into the room with two big duffel bags, shoving them in Fats' and Big Face's arms saying, "We give ya this for saving us life, we thank ya greatly, now go... go fast!"

While his mother repeated, "Thank ya for saving us life, thank ya for saving us life..." she grabbed another duffel that was full of money from behind the refrigerator and shoved it to her son. Then she yelled, "Kabiru, ya go now!"

He ran off with the duffel bag so they fled in the opposite direction. With shit moving so fast and Fats bleeding they never looked inside the duffel bags until back at the spot with Kareem and Teno, who was still at the table mixing the dope.

When the zippers were pulled back revealing pounds of weed, jars of ecstasy pills, and ounces of lean which is a mix of codeine and prometazine, they knew why dude drug her old ass to the kitchen and realized these Nigerians were moving some heavy weight.

They only got down with heavys with the exceptions of a few small customers to keep a feel of the streets. Fats yelled, "Shit... I should of body-bagged pissy boy and took the other bag with all the money... fuck!"

Big Face told him, "Fats, they think we did all that for them. They don't realize it was only cause our lives was in danger too. Don't trip, you see the hustle god just blessed us with the rest of the package... it's officially E.S.B, or die baby!"

The E.S.B was now like 31 Flavors. In a few days, they recruited workers and opened up shop in Terror Town with the coke, cush weed in the B's, ecstasy and lean in the Jeffery Manor maze, and in the back of the Manor known as The Back they laid the dope down. This put E.S.B on the map with their names coming off many tongues far and near.

The Nigerians, out of gratitude, began feeding them for unbelievable prices. The Nigerians and Kevo pipeline on the coke and dope equaled a solid connect all around the board.

Their daily scene and activities suddenly changed. The trap houses were moving like they had revolving doors. Zombied-out cluckers was flooding the spots. Coke and dope was being smoked, snorted, and poked in many veins. Tons of young people copped and popped ecstasy pills, rolling, living fantasy life like it was real. Pounds of cush weed was being inhaled, leaving a smoke that had you stuck in mode feeling crucial. Ounces of lean were being drunk making the world turn slow like it was all just a dream. Workers and fiends made hand-to-hand exchanges. Security was cocking choppers and doing pat downs, yelling, "Five, 0!" Money was being folded, stacked, and wrapped in rubber bands. This all resulted in the E.S.B pulling up in the clubs parking lot with new whips, equipped with T.V's, flossing wet paint jobs, riding on chrome six's and eight's, which is a term for 26 and 28 inch rims. Climbing out their whips with next year Pelle Pelles wrapped around their backs. Jewels around their necks glistening in the light. The baddest bitches bending over spreading their cheeks and dropping to their knees. Yeah, they finally came up. But it still wasn't enough for all them to eat right. They wasn't flipping near what they should be flipping. The numbers weren't right because of all the competitors in the game.

Narrator, Lucifer

There's nothing like black unity huh? It seems like every groups purpose change when that all mighty dollar god come to join or shall we say to plug in. No group can survive without him joining, that's why the E.S.B, went to recruit that all mighty devil. But once you let him join and he moves up in the ranks, taking the title as the ruler of all evil, I guarantee that all of hell is soon to break loose. But don't worry, it won't break loose until he let his brothers greed and envy join. Aye, now you see why I love this shit. Move bitch get out the way.

Chapter 3

A lot of hustlers who was getting real money started to drop in on a local dice game in the parking lot of White Castle on 79th and South Chicago. The Eastside Brothers decided to drop in so they could get a feel of the competition and let their presences be known. While they rolled through the dice game flossing what they earning in a flip-flop red and blue painted Dodge Durango on some chrome 32 inch rims, they let their cush smoke filled eyes stalk the crowd threw the tented windows like vultures.

Teno said, "Ain't that Chuck on the dice who run that spot for Mann?"

Big Face replied, "Yeah, that's why we can't come up, cause that dike-bitch Mann getting all the fucking money!"

They parked and jumped out the truck letting their diamond cluster E.S.B. chains hang and swing from around their necks as they stomped in the mist of the crowd continuing to let their eyes stalk the crowd that was filled with hustlers who get dirty money and the baddest bitches in town who prey on squeezing them dry. Once Fats pulled out a wad of money and started fading the dice game, Kareem grabbed a thick red bone female by the arm and began to sweet talk her as Big Face and Teno started saying sweet nothings to her two pretty girlfriends.

Suddenly, Mann, a big yellow dike female, snuck up and started pistol-whipping Chuck, who was on his knees rolling the dice. Mann dug in Chucks, pockets, took all his money out and said, "Bitch, where the rest of my money at?" as the crowd began to disappear one of Chuck buddies ran up flashing a gun at Mann, so Mann let Chuck go and said to his buddy, "Nigga, I'll fuck you!"

Then Mann shot him four times in the stomach before running off. Everyone quickly evacuated while Mann burned out in her purple Bentley G.T, fleeing the scene. The area was soon empty with just Chuck and his buddy laying in White Castle's parking lot on the ground bleeding.

Mann

Mann is a five foot nine inch, 267-pound, chunky yellow complexion, black female with long braids. She got the name Mann because she's a dike who look just like a man. Some people don't even know she's a female. She got a few murders under her belt which is the reason why many men are scared of her. Mann's checking major paper supplying the south and east side with cocaine and cush weed. Big Face and Teno use to cop their drugs from her. Mann is in the Pyramid gang from 61st and Woods. She keep the baddest bitches, everyone want to fuck, as her girlfriends. The crazy part is they be chasing her, but she falls in love too easy and will kill you over one of them hoes.

After the show-and-tell at the dice game that Mann shut down, the eyes of the streets began to observe the E.S.B. popping tags, flipping whips, blowing fifty thousand at dice games, and each drug spot checking double digit stacks every night. This resulted in all the different gangs they were in to start hating on them.

During this time, in some parts of Chicago, a member from another gang was allowed to hustle in their area if it benefited them. This was under conditions set by the Chief. So now, unlike the early 1990's, different gangs would get together to perform criminal activities until a war broke out with that gang.

Coincidently, each one of them were summoned to a mandatory meeting with their Board member, Prince, and Five Star General Chief. At these meetings, they were told that they were allowing the opposition to eat off their land which was taking food out the mouth of their own gang. Their Chiefs also threatened to classify them as an enemy and to deal with them violently if a tax wasn't paid weekly.

Later when the E.S.B finally met back up with each other and found out that they all had experienced a similar extortion alternative Teno said, "I ain't going for that shit, we the E.S.B. now. We is the mob. We don't need them no more."

Big Face stated, "This ain't the early 90's, they got it fucked up. We don't honor them bitches. We renegades. We kill Chiefs."

Fats said, "Off with the Head's heads then!"

"I don't give a fuck, I'm down for whatever, fam. It's E.S.B or die with me. We ain't part of their little gangs no more." Kareem said.

A meeting of the minds took place with a deceptive plot ending in bloodshed of the gangs they were once loyal to for the rise of the E.S.B. who they would now die for.

Big Face's last comment was, "They our competition. If they were out the way we could get rich."

Fats paid Spook a Dave Chappelle-looking dude who was the five-star General that controlled his area a couple of pounds of cush for his taxation. Then Spook had the Legions selling the cush on 86th Street between Marquette and Burham to catch customers before they got to Fats' spot on Burham.

Meanwhile, during the day Teno managed to get a 350 pound, black dude name Big 'B', who was the driver for Prince Zulu to take him to get some weed from 86th Street, before taking him the tax money he had for him.

Prince Zulu the Prince over the area of Terror Town for the Pyramids had a head full of dreadlocks.

Big 'B' turned on 86th Street. The Legions knew Prince Zulu would be reclined in the passenger seat, while Big 'B' drove him around in the red Lincoln Navigator truck with black tent, riding 32 inch chrome rims. They greeted them by throwing up the fist - a common symbol both their gangs shared.

One shorty called Young Legion ran up to the truck to sell them an ounce of cush. After the transaction, Big 'B' rolled the tented windows back up and passed Teno the weed.

Teno switched the weed with a bogus ounce and told Big 'B', "Go back and give this shit back to shorty, they trying to go on us... Look at this shit, Big 'B'."

They then pulled back on 86th Street and began to argue with Young Legion until Big 'B' got frustrated and threw the weed back at shorty and said, "You can keep that shit, shorty. It's nothing to me. Now go buy your broke ass something pretty with it nigga." Then he pulled off. Ten minutes later, an identical truck rolled down 86th Street shooting non-stop shots killing Young Legion and another one of the shorty Legions as they tried to run in a cut away between two houses.

Now Young Legion, who was to graduate from Bowen High school this year, will never get the chance to touch a diploma. Neither will his friend who was a sophomore and honor roll student at C.V.S High school.

Once Spook heard about the incident, he called a meeting of all the Legion with Fats in attendance. The Legions and the Pyramids in this area had a reported history of going to war with each other leaving death tolls high on each side.

The Legions had a small territory in the center of the Pyramids' area. They were greatly outnumbered but held their land down firmly, gaining respect from all. Once Fats told Spook he had an idea where they might be later, Spook figured he could avoid a war by hitting them directly and fast with no one suspecting them. Before the News could make coverage of the murder on 86th Street, Spook was leading his best go-getters to hit Big 'B' and Prince Zulu, as they pulled in an empty gas station on 75th and Yates.

Once Spook gave the signal for a car to quickly pull up in front and one beside the truck, blocking them in by a gas pump, Big 'B' who had already gotten out and made it to the passenger side, noticed the car coming and instantly got to firing shots from an automatic hand gun.

However, the sidecar rolled up shooting a sawed off 12 gauge pump that knocked his face off - it would be a closed casket for him.

While this was happening, Prince Zulu shot his 45 Desert Eagle through the truck's front window. But it was no match, because the car in front let an A.K. 47 ride that killed him leaving his dreadlocks slumped over on the dashboard; he was still clutching his pistol.

After that, the only sounds heard was screams from a lady cashier in the gas station and super charged engines that spent burning tires as they fled the scene.

Once days went by and Spook got word the Mids had no idea who did it, he considered the hit a success and raised Fats rank to a three star General.

A couple days later in the Jeffery Manor maze Kareem radars was on high alert as he re-upped the drug houses. When he jumped back in his Dodge Charger he noticed Mann ride by in her black Range Rover with the black rims, so off instinct he instantly followed. From half a block away he watched Mann pull up to Ron's house with Joe-Joe jumping out holding a large duffel bag, rushing into the house. As Mann pulled off, Kareem's gut told him to just sit and wait. That s when he witnessed Joe-Joe with the same bag and Ron come out the side door to enter the garage. Kareem then rolled a blunt and sat on the spot for a little over an hour when Joe-Joe pulled out the garage in a candy apple green Grand National, with custom made one of a kind 28 inch rims that had the G.M. symbol on the hood. He parked it across the street and went back into the house. Kareem then got out the Charger ducking low and within 60 seconds he was pulling off with Joe-Joe's whip, while texting Big Face to meet him at the spot in Terror Town.

Joe-Joe, who looked just like Rick Ross the rapper, was a Board member over the Manor and a few other areas out east for the Goblin gang. Ron, who is a muscular dude who look like Booker T. the wrestler, was Joe-Joe's flunky who did whatever he said, so he gave him some rank as the region over the Manor.

When Big Face pulled up, Kareem, like a frantic little kid, told him, "Look in the garage."

Big Face, with a surprised look on his face said, "Why the fuck is Joe-Joe shit here?"

Kareem replied, "I jacked him at a stop sign. Naw, I'm just playing. I took it because I seen him with Mann and I think he got some shit stashed in it."

Big Face replied, "Yeah, he been making runs to Iowa and Minnesota. He got a few spots down there he be feeding. Where Teno at? Call Fats right now. They ain't gone believe this shit."

Once Teno and Fats got there, they began to take the car apart. When Teno got the dash board loose and found 20 kilos of cocaine he yelled, "Hallelujah." Satan's deceptive plot was now in motion."

Spook owned a bootleg rim shop on 79th and Manistee. This particular night, just before closing time, he watched a dirty old dope fiend man come in rolling some rims.

The dope fiend said, "Hey man, just give me $200 for em'."

Spook eyes got big as he checked out the sparkling rims as he realized they were some one-of-a-kind exclusives he could sell for at least five thousand easy. He put his game face on and said, "Where you get these rims from? I don't want no stolen shit."

The dope fiend said, "My nephew went to jail and told me to sell them for bond money."

Spook told him, "I'll give you $175 for that bullshit, that's it."

He responded, "Sold!"

Spook, who was excited to now have the rims that were sparkling, set them in the display window before locking up for the night.

The dope fiend who was also excited rushed to the dope house for Big Face to give him his reward. Big Face knew a dead man can't talk plus a dope fiend dying off a jab of heroin would pump up business for the spot in the back. So, he gave him a jab of poison that left him dead before sunrise. Once the word got out that the dope killed, the daily numbers doubled.

Much later that night, Kareem and Fats broke into Spook's rim shop through the roof. Once inside, they planted five kilos of cocaine in the shop's display speaker. When exiting the shop these dudes repatched the roof like nothing ever happened.

Joe-Joe had Ron alert all his guys that a reward was out for whoever found his car. Once Big Face and Kareem heard about this, they went to talk to Joe-Joe face-to-face.

Big Face then told him, "This hook-ass nigga from the B's, my man Fats put me up on, was trying to sell us some coke for the low-low, so we went to his rim shop to holla at him. Soon as I walked in I seen some rims that looked just like yours."

Big Face didn't say nothing else after that so Joe-Joe asked, "Did ya'll fuck with the nigga?"

He responded, "Hell naw, that nigga had me thinking he was trying to set us up with the police when he got to pulling birds out a speaker he had in the shop. I hurried up and told that nigga we was straight and got the fuck up out of there. But when I heard that your shit got stolen, I said them might be 'G' rims."

Then Joe-Joe loudly stated, "Ron, you just heard that shit? Go get some of the guys. We about to go holla at dude!"

Twenty minutes later Joe-Joe and Ron, and four of the Goblins walked into the rim shop. Ron asked the lady working in the shop, "Could you please go get the owner for me?"

She said, "Alright." Then, she went in the back room and came back out with Spook and two of his guys.

Now, as Joe-Joe stared at the rims in the display window he said, "How much you want for them rims? I got to have them."

Spook said, "Five stacks."

That's when Ron pulled out a Mac-11 while four of the Goblins pulled out and cocked choppers.

"Come off that shit partner," Joe-Joe said.

Spook replied, "Ya'll must don't know who the fuck I am for ya'll to be making a bad decision like robbing me."

Joe-Joe grabbed the display speaker off the wall and busted it open and pulled five keys of coke out and yelled, "You mutha fucka, where's the rest of my shit?"

Spook knew some bullshit was going on so he pulled out his Glock nine millimeter and busted a couple shots off as he dove behind the counter with Lisa his cashier.

The Legions pulled out some automatic handguns and busted a few shots but the Goblins with them choppers made their bodies knock over a pile of rims and tires before dying.

Next, Ron ran behind the counter firing off that Mac 11 but Spook grabbed Lisa using her body as a shield. Spook shot Ron twice causing him to stumble and drop his gun.

One of the Goblins came from the other side of the counter and gave him five shots to the back of the head.

As Joe-Joe grabbed the coke he yelled, "Shit, ya'll wasn't suppose to kill him until I got the rest of my shit. Grab them rims so we can get the fuck up out of here."

Joe-Joe knew he had to find a way to make up for them fifteen keys he lost so he started to put the pressure on Big Face and Kareem for that tax money.

At the ecstasy and lean spot in the Manor maze Big Face told the E.S.B, "The next nigga Joe-Joe send over here talking about where that shit at or shut it down, we gone shut and lay they ass down."

Then Teno said, "Look at this shit." As he turned the volume up on the 54 inch flat screen TV that was showing the W.G.N Midday News,

Kareem stated, "That's little Jemarion on the News."

Big Face said, "Where you see him at?"

He replied, "That's him with the blue Polo shirt on looking stupid. Fenger High school ain't no joke, another shorty just got shot up at his school today." Fats then stated, "That's all the high schools now. Shit, even the little grammar schoolers getting it in now."

Little Jemarion, was a kid from the Manor who went to school every day got good grades, and stayed out of trouble. Little Jemarion, like many other kids in the hood, could barely afford shoes on their feet let long bus fare to get to school. For this kid, hustling was the only solution to his problem so he asked Kareem to put him on. Kareem gave him a job at the ecstasy and lean spot working second shift after school. Now an hour and a half later he was reporting in for work, giving his account of the incident at Fenger High. He told everyone that was standing outside in front of the trap house, "I was at the bus stop when I saw a crowd around a fight so I ran up busting through the crowd to see if it was one of the J.M.G's. When it wasn't, I started hollering at Alexis, that's this thick chocolate girl who be sweating a pimp, when all of a sudden this dude got to shooting. So I grabbed her like, come on girl, I got you and threw her to the ground and laid on top of her to keep her safe."

He was interrupted by another kid saying, "Nigga, stop lying, we seen your scary ass on the News. You was laying on the ground scared to death with the bitch laying on top of you. Then they showed you running to the bus stop leaving the bitch behind."

They all started to laugh at him. A few kids who knew the boy who got killed at school began to speak their peace of how he was a good dude who this shouldn't of happen to.

Jemarion walked over to the driveway where the E.S.B was standing around a Dodge Charger and said, "I ain't going back to school no more. Fuck school. I'm ready to be out here like ya'll getting it in, checking a grip. Let me run this spot for ya'll. I want to be just like ya'll."

Big Face told him, "Trust me, shorty, you don't wanta be like us. This the only way for us. You, you got a lot of ways to make it in this life. Don't fuck that up. We need you to be our lawyer when we catch a case, our doctor for when we get shot up, and our banker to launder and wash our money. So go to school little nigga. Plus, you know our rules; if you don't go to school and pass your classes, you can't work or get no money out here."

He looked at Big Face with a funny face and said, "Nigga is you crazy, you tripping, I'm out here."

He responded, "You must ain't hear me huh?"

He replied, "I ain't trying to hear that shit."

Big Face grabbed him by the throat and held him up in the air as he squeezed his windpipe and said, "Can you hear me now! If I ever catch you out here again, I'm gonna murk you myself. If I hear you ain't at school, or even getting bad grades, I'm gonna send them goons for your head. Now do you understand?"

As Jemarion fought for air to remain conscience, Big Face stuffed eight thousand dollars in his pockets, which was some money he just collected from a worker. Then he let him go and watched him run off down the street. Fats, laughing said, "I heard of strong arm robbery but not strong arm charity. How you gonna choke a little nigga then put money in his pockets? That's crazy!"

Teno, who was also laughing said, "They gone give your ass a child abuse case."

Fats jumped back in saying, "How you gone explain, you choked a little boy then put money in his pockets? That sound real kinky. They gone slam your ass, then have you register with them pedophilies for touching on people's kids."

Kareem wasn't laughing because he knew better than anyone why he did what he did.

Moments later, Ron pulled up in a Chevy Caprice four deep, jumping out telling them, "I finally caught all ya'll together. Let me holla at ya'll inside." as they all went inside the trap house Kareem patted the top of his head, which was a code to let the block security men know to shut the block down. That meant make everybody leave, shut down incoming traffic, and for them to be the only one's on the block who were posted out of sight in sniper mode.

Now once they were all in the spot Kareem said, "We was waiting on you to come personally and grab these endz. You know we ain't about to put shit in nobody else hands... Just hold on, I'll be right back." He then went upstairs.

Teno and Fats sat on the couch and began to play N.B.A. 2K11, on the giant flat screen TV, Teno said to the Goblins with Ron, "I'm the best at this. I'll double anything ya'll put up."

Two of the Goblins were sitting on the couch with them to see how their game was, while Big Face fake-kicked it with Ron and another one of the Goblins.

Big Face asked Ron, "Did ya'll go holla at dude and see if them was fam rims?"

Ron responded, "We went through there, but them wasn't his rims so we left."

"What happened to your arm?" Big Face asked.

"I got it wrapped up cause I just got some new tattoos," Ron said.

Teno next asked Ron, "What you know about this here?"

"I don't play games!" Ron said while looking at the guys he brought with him with a mean mug on his face. "We ain't come here to play!"

Kareem came down the stairs with a Nike shoe box that he had given to Ron. When he opened the shoe box, it did what it was supposed to do – it exploded in Ron's face. The gas from the explosion left him temporary blinded.

The whole time Teno and Fats were sitting on the couch they had their guns concealed and aimed under the couch pillows at the two guys on the couch with them. So, when the shoe box exploded, their guns also exploded with bullets busting through the pillows to their company's chest as cotton flew all around the room.

While Ron couldn't see, Big Face hit him in the eye and put him in the sleeper choke hold. The other guy managed to shoot his way out the house against Teno's and Fats shots only to get sniped down by one of the block security men.

Kareem rushed to drag his body back inside the house.

When Ron woke up, he was in the basement tied up to a chair naked. Teno and Fats tortured Ron for about an hour trying to get Joe-Joe's whereabouts, but he wouldn't give up no information. Then, Fats grabbed some big tree branch cutters and said, "One of ya'll grab his dick so I can cut it off."

They all protested, "I ain't grabbing shit!" They argued for about thirty minutes until Fats got mad and recklessly cut it off, then shoved it in his victim's mouth as he told him, "Eat this you prick ass nigga."

Then they gasolined the spot and had a security man set it a flame as they rode off.

They were now on the hunt for Joe-Joe. They knew if they didn't kill him soon there would be a big bloody war that would decline their inclining business.

The next day, they found out that while Ron was eating his own penis, Joe-Joe was on I-55 getting bumped off by the Feds for trying to take five kilos of cocaine and some assault weapons to Minnesota. They knew the Manor would be hot as a fire, crawling with Homicide Detectives, so they decided to lay low by packing up a nice amount of ecstasy and lean to hit N.I.U. campus where Kareem getting ready to start with his full basketball scholarship.

Narrator, Lucifer

Move bitch get out the way! Aye, I see once they were done stunting they let that damn spirit of greed plug in. This nigga came in the door eliminating the competition for his chief money, the ruler of all evil. They may not be honoring their old chief, but if their new chief say shut em down watch how fast they shut em' down. Are these role models your kids have drug dealers, like Mann, killers, and dope fiends? It's no wonder why the shorties mastering the murder game now. But if you like it I love it. Now as far as that truck that killed them young Legions, naw Big 'B', and Prince Zulu wasn't behind it. Shit, they didn't even know a truck like theirs rode through shooting. For the record, let's just say the E.S.B, know who did it. Well, they just got their hands dirty cleaning the path, now they got to lay low. But let's see if they can under my influence. Until we meet again, Lucifer G.

Chapter 4

As a red Tahoe truck rode around on the campus of N.I.U. with the E.S.B. reclined in its seats. Big Face said, "This where we relocating the spot at... it's prefect. We can do what we do in the city, then come here to check on Kareem and lay low, fucking bitches off 'X' all day while getting some slow head off that lean.." He then instructed Kareem, Look little brother, make your main focus school and making it to the N.B.A. draft. I don't want you touching shit but money. Make the workers work." Within a few days time they had Kareem running an ecstasy and lean spot right off campus, with seventy-five percent of their customers young freaky schoolgirls looking for action.

While they were on campus helping Kareem get settled in, two white girls approached them with one saying, "Hi, I'm Amie, here's an invitation to my party tonight; you mustn't miss it for anything in the world. If I don't see you guys there, me and my girls will come hunt you down, so you all better show up."

They brushed them off with no thoughts of going to their party until that night when the off campus trap house sold out from a flood of young partygoers. Then they knew they had to go see what all the fuss was about.

As the chrome, Ashanti grill glistened on the candy apple red Tahoe that the E.S.B. pulled up in, spectators stared at the shiny 32 inch rims as they spun then came to a sudden stop in front of the house party. The E.S.B. was filled with amazement when they witnessed the site of a two-story house packed with people partying inside, outside all on the porch, all around on the lawn, and all out in the street.

The street was like a car show with chrome rims sparkling, Lamborghini doors up, TV screens flashing, with sounds bumping having a parking lot pimping party on front street. Once they finally made their way into the actually house party, they was packed in with college kids of all origins, who were heavily influenced off cush weed, lean, and ecstasy pills. They watched a group of girls who wore their sorority shirts do a dance ritual for a few minutes before they got to parlaying in the party, once they began to lay their mack game down to some Asian, African, Latino, and even some Australian girls, a white girl walked up to Kareem and said, "My girls want you and your friends to come talk to them."

He replied, "Where they at?"

She said, "Follow me," as she led them into the kitchen area with four other girls.

As Big Face walked into the kitchen, he seen the two girls who invited them to the party and said, "Aye ya'll, it's the snow bunnies from earlier. I couldn't wait to come party with ya'll. Now can me and my guys go to the V.I.P. section with ya'll or what?"

One of the girls responded, "I was hoping you would say that. We want you guys to come to the after party with us."

Another one of her girls spoke up, "It's already started, you all better come on."

Teno seen a sink full of ice and drinks and said, "We got the 'X' and cush, ya'll grab them drinks and we up."

After they grabbed the drinks, all five girls led them out the back door to a house next door where another party had already begun.

Once they stood in the living room of the house next door and realized they were in the middle of an orgy party, they looked at each other with surprised looks and thought to themselves - this is paradise.

As the girls closed the door behind them, Big Face, with a smile on his face, witnessed a naked girl laying on top of another girl kissing, while a third girl ate the girl on top's pussy from behind.

Kareem eyes witnessed a guy lying on the rug getting rode by one girl while another sat on his face as they kissed each other.

Fats, with a disgusted look on his face, witnessed three guys running a train on one girl on the couch. They were sandwiching her while a third guy stood over them getting a blow job.

Fats said, "Aye snow bunnies, we ain't on that." As he handed Big Face some condoms. He leaned in to whisper, "Don't let them joints bust. You give my sister something, I'm cutting yours off too."

Teno saw a girl bent over on a love seat getting fucked from the back.

Then the girls took them to a master bedroom upstairs.

As Teno walked into the big bedroom, he pulled out a camera and said, "Alright snow bunnies, it's show time. This ya'll big debut. I want ya'll best performance."

Two of the girls then grabbed Teno taking him into a bathroom connected to the room where they pulled his jeans down with one putting his dick in her mouth while the other sucked on his balls.

Kareem said, "How he get two?"

The girls looked over from the bathroom and said, "We're going to lick all ya'll like a lolly pop."

They all blazed up some cush weed, popped 'X' pills, and drank while they performed different sex acts.

One of the girls bent over on a dresser, spread her butt cheeks, and began to beg Kareem saying, "Please Daddy, put it up my ass."

Big Face jokingly yelled, "Kobe Bryant, don't do it!" as he plunged into her, fucking her in the ass as she moaned and screamed, "Fuck me good, you big-dick, black muthafucka you!"

While Fats was on the bed busy fucking one of the girls from the back, ramming her head into the head board. Big Face picked one of the girls up in the air making her wrap her legs around his waist. As she bounced up and down on his dick, he stood up holding her by the ass cheeks until she tried to kiss him. That's when he turned his head away and dropped her to the floor stating, "I don't do that... Aye Teno, time to switch homie."

Teno made the girl Big Face was just fucking bend over to touch her toes as he opened her pussy lips up and said, "Aye ya'll look. This how a pink-toe look when you crack it open."

Meanwhile, Big Face was in the bathroom watching the two girls tongue kiss and take turns putting his dick in their mouths, one of the girls then swallowed his whole dick while the other one swallowed his balls, making him let out a loud grunting noise. While he grunted, she pulled his dick out her wet mouth and the two girls just looked up at him as he sat partly on the sink shaking as he came in their faces. Then, he watched them lick it off each other's face and the rest of his dick as he sat on the sink shaking in fulfillment.

After they all took turns videotaping the white girls sucking them up and getting fucked by them, they robbed the girls of their valuables while they laid passed out all over the room. They took I-pods, jewelry, money, and cell phones. This was just a ritual they did when they ran through some hoes as a trademark.

Then, Big Face looked at all his guys and said, "Do any of ya'll know these bitches names?"

With confused looks on their faces, they shook their heads side to side stating, "I don't know... It's snow bunny ain't it?"

The orgy was over and they were now back in business mode. They knew they had to get back to the city to re-coop more drugs, so they snuck out the house, leaving the snow bunnies naked laying passed out and robbed with their pussies, asses, and mouths sore.

Narrator, Lucifer

Yeah, it's your boy again, the spirit of Err A.K.A. Lucifer. All I got to say is if these business incline hustlers ain't have to go re-up their supply they would of still been trapped in ecstasy indulging in its lust with them snow bunnies. Also, I love them dumb Chicago niggas like Kareem who got a talent that gives him a key to a better life but willing to fuck it up chasing street dreams. I'll be counting for eternity if I counted all the potential N.B.A, N.F.L, Rappers, Singers, and etc. who almost made it but fucked it up living that Chi-Town gangsta life. But fuck all that. What's crazy is, if you call pumping a dope house up off campus laying low while having orgies, I'll hate to see how you draw attention then telling Kareem to focus on school.

The power of confusion I love it. But now I guess it's back to the city for another episode, huh? Let's root for more sex, drugs, money, and murder.

Chapter 5

Kareem was finally finished filling out all his paperwork on campus and wasn't due back for another week, so he rode back to the city to help re-up from their supplier and process the drugs. While they were riding back, they made a few calls to check on their drug houses and workers. They got news that Joe-Joe was out around town making moves.

Fats said, "That nigga couldn't have bonded out that quick... something ain't right."

Then Big Face said, "We still gone get his ass but first we got to get this work."

The E.S.B, went to Big Face house who stayed in a condo downtown with his girlfriend Keshia and daughter Alivia. As they all walked in through the front door, his daughter ran up to him saying, "Hey Daddy. Where you been? I miss you."

After he hugged and kissed her, he said, "I miss you too Boo. Daddy was working. Where's your momma at?"

She replied, "In the room Daddy."

"Alivia come give your Uncle a hug," Fats said.

When Big Face walked in the room with Keshia, a six-inch Stiletto came flying across the room missing his head by inches. He quickly closed the door to the bedroom as Keshia yelled, "You ain't gone keep leaving us for days like this and why the fuck you ain't answer my calls or return my messages? You must think I'm a punk or something. Nigga guard your grill, I'm about to show you who the punk is."

While she danced around the room like a Boxer Big Face said, "You know I ain't about to fight you."

She responded, "Well you about to get knocked out like a punk bitch then."

Kareem heard them arguing so he turned the TV up in the living room until it drowned them out.

Back in the bedroom, Keshia swung a right fist that hit him in the left eye. He then rushed, charging her and grabbing her, throwing her to the bed and pinning her down. As he held her down on the bed, he pulled the little shorts and panties down she had on.

She looked at him as she fought to get loose and said, "Nigga, let me go so I can beat your ass. You ain't getting none cause I'm still mad at you."

Once he got her little shorts and panties all the way down, he unhooked his belt buckle, pulled out his hard, erect dick, and stuck it between her legs.

As his dick slid inside her already-wet pussy, she stopped fighting and made an "ooooooh" sound before saying, "O.K, baby, I ain't mad at you no more. Just make sure you answer all my calls from now on.

He replied, "Shut up!" and began rapildly pounding away as she wrapped her legs around his back, squeezing her pussy around his dick, throwing that pussy back at him, pumping back with his motions until three minutes, later when they both came together.

As they laid deep into each other kissing they heard a glass break in the kitchen then Alivia crying, "Ooooowa, I'm telling my mommy uncle Fats is breaking her stuff."

Keshia pushed Big Face up off her, put on her shorts and robe, and ran out the room yelling, "Fats, I'm gone beat your ass like how I use to when we was little, because I told you to stay out my kitchen."

Big Face went into the living room where Teno and Kareem were counting some money they had out covering the coffee table. He sat down in a leather recliner, laid back, grabbed a phone, dialed Kevo number and said, "You watch that W.N.B.A, game?"

"My girl Sophia Young shot their lights out, didn't she? I told you they was gone cover that spread," Big Face said.

"Yeah, she did her thang, but what you think she gone do when they play the Chicago Sky?" asked Kevo.

"She gone double them numbers on that game, Homie. Just watch!" Big Face said.

Kevo asked, "So you willing to double our usual bet on that?"

Big Face quickly responded, "Yup!"

Then Kevo said, "Since your team at home, I ain't gone watch it until half time. So, it's a bet, Homie. I'll holla at you then."

They hung up and then Big Face made another call.

When the old Nigerian lady answered he said, "Hey Grandma, could you make me some that jerk chicken with some sweet tea and my favorite desert?"

In an accent she answered, "Baby whenever you get hungry, come get Granny's good food.

He said, "I'll be there for dinner."

"Baby, this time ya don't bring me no pound of frosting just bring half of that," Granny told him. "Ya don't have to bring nothing right now, I'll still cook for ya baby."

He replied, "See you later then granny."

"O.K, bye bye, baby," Granny said before hanging up.

Both phones then hung up.

The Feds had just planted fresh wiretaps on Big Face phone at his condo and was excited to interpret his recent calls. Federal Agent Muhad Shabazz interpreted his first conversation with Kevo to really be:

> Big Face: Didn't I tell you we was gone run through that last package.
>
> Kevo: What you need now?
>
> Big Face: We need double what we got last time.
>
> Kevo: So you got double the money?

Big Face: Yup!

Kevo: I'm gone bring it to your house around twelve
O'clock holla at you.

He also interpreted the conversation with the Nigerian lady to
really be:

Big Face: Hey, Grandma I need some more weed, lean,
and 'X' pills.

Old Lady: When ya gone come pick it up?

Big Face: Later on tonight.

Old lady: Ya don't have to bring me the full price this
time. I only want half for it. Ya really don't have to
bring me nothing right now, I got ya.

Big Face: See you later then granny.

Old lady: OK, bye bye, baby.

Agent Muhad Shabazz was a dedicated Muslim and community
activist who grew up on the eastside of Chicago. He was dedicated to
rebuilding his community so he got involved in law- enforcement. He
had a few run-ins with the E.S.B, each individually many years ago
when he was a gang and drug task force Detective working at 103rd,
71st, and other eastside police stations. Now that the Feds had launched
a full investigation on the E.S.B, along with a few other groups from
out east, it was his job to take them down.

The phone conversations were the first big lead on them but

couldn't be considered one hundred percent accurate. It was just an assumption plus their whereabouts was unknown. What agent Muhad didn't know, but found out for sure, was the E.S.B. were linked to Kevo.

Kevo had been on his radar for a long time. Now, he was close to taking him down with the E.S.B. being next on his hit list.

It was now one P.M. and Kevo hadn't showed up yet. This wasn't like Kevo, Big Face thought to himself as he reclined on his sofa while his guys played Playstation and Keshia cooked lunch. He knew if Kevo said twelve o'clock, that's what he meant. He knew Kevo made all his runs during the early day and usually wrapped it up by two o'clock.

He began to get frustrated as he called and left numerous messages for him only to get no response. The workers were out of work plus he was anxious to hit the drug table to get it all done with.

A few hours went by with still no show from Kevo. It was time to go meet the old lady, so Big Face told Kareem and Teno, "Ya'll fall back here in case Kevo comes through or something. We about to go holla at the old lady."

***

Two days before the E.S.B. came back from N.I.U., Kevo sat reclined, hidden behind tented windows, smoking some cush weed in his all white Benz, as he swerved through traffic, banging through the speakers a Rick Ross song, "I think I'm Big Meech, Larry Hoover, whipping work, Hallelujah, One nation, Under God, Real Niggas get money from the fuckin' start."

When he pulled into the car wash on 67th and South Chicago, he saw Joe-Joe flagging him down.

Joe-Joe had been riding around town for two days looking for Kevo. He knew there was three places he could catch him at if he was lucky and those spots were the basketball court on 98th and Yates, a restaurant on 79th and Western, or the car wash on 67th and South Chicago. He had already ridden by the other two spots and was now at the carwash waiting to get his car detailed when he sighted Kevo waiting to get his car detailed.

Once Kevo seen him, he jumped out to shake Joe-Joe's hand. Joe-Joe said, "What's good fam? I been trying to catch you for a few days now. I know we ain't never did no business or nothing, but you got that shit the streets dying from. The stud I was fucking with don't got that killer. So, you know me, I got to be on the winning team."

Kevo use to play in the basketball tournaments that he used to sponsor when he had N.B.A. hoop dreams. He was well familiar with Joe-Joe's high ranking status in the streets for the Goblin gang. He also knew supplying him meant a business opportunity that would double his business. Kevo, now being anxious to make the deal, told him, "You already know by it being you I got you for the low-low, but you got to keep fucking with me."

Joe-Joe responded, "How fast can you have ten books of heroin and thirty books of coke for me, cause I got to hit the highway. I got people waiting on me."

"Give me your number. I'll have you on the highway in no longer than two days," Kevo told Joe-Joe.

Joe-Joe said, "We good then."

Kevo then asked, "What you up here getting armored all down? I know you love them old schools. Is you up here in that Grand National?"

He laughed and said, "You think you know me huh? I lost that one. That's my Chevellele with the flip flop red and blue paint he just brought out."

They exchanged numbers then Joe-Joe said, "I got a few moves to make. I'll holla." Then, he jumped in his Chevellele, but before pulling off he told Kevo, "Tell em' to spray some of that kiwi air freshener in your shit, it's the bomb partner."

TWO days later Kevo was at B.P. gas station that he owned on the corner of 95th and King Drive. He was putting together some coke and dope to drop off to the E.S.B. while he waited on Joe-Joe to come make their transaction.

Joe-Joe arrived in his Chevelle jumping out with a duffel bag in his hand.

Kevo met him at the front door.

Joe-Joe unzipped the bag revealing a large amount of money, then gave it to Kevo saying, "That's all the cash, Mr. Ice Cream man."

They went to get into an old Omni car where Kevo revealed the stashed kilos. When they got out, Kevo threw him the keys to the car.

Suddenly, out of nowhere, over a dozen marked, and unmarked, police cars pulled up on them from King Drive. Federal agents jumped out pointing guns yelling, "Freeze F.B.I. Put your hands up!"

When they put their hands up, Kevo yelled, "What you bitches want? My lawyers not gon like how you hoes harassing me and my company."

Agent Shabazz then stated, "Good job, Joe-Joe."

Kevo looked at Joe-Joe who was now putting his hands down and said, "Say it ain't so Joe-Joe, say it ain't fucking so, tell me it ain't fucking so, you muthafucka."

Joe-Joe looked at him and said, "It was either you or me and I chose you, partner." Kevo then quickly threw the duffel bag that was around his shoulders, still unzipped at the crowd of Feds. As money flew in the air, Kevo grabbed a nine Bretta hand gun from his waist and put it to Joe-Joe s head. He then told the Feds, "I'm gone push this bitch brains out if you hoes don't let me drive away in that car."

Joe-Joe being a much larger man than Kevo decided to try his luck, so he ducked and pushed Kevo to the ground then ran westbound towards traffic on 95th Street.

Kevo jumped up to chase him down while the Feds took off in pursuit after him.

As Joe-Joe ran down 95th Street in the middle of traffic, Kevo recklessly started shooting at him. Kevo, being an athlete, weaved through traffic and jumped over cars to catch up to him.

When Joe-Joe tried to pull a lady out of her car, he let loose a few more shots, that all struck him in the side of his body making him fall to the ground.

When Kevo ran up with his nine millimeter aimed at Joe-Joe's head and squeezed, the gun just clicked. It was out of bullets, so he jumped on top of him and began pistol-whipping him until the Feds tackled and pulled him off Joe.

As the Feds drug Kevo away, his shouts got lower and lower until he couldn't be heard no more yelling,

"On my word, I'm gone kill your ass, Joe-Joe. My money too long. I'm bonding out tonight, plus I'm putting a milly up on your head for whoever bring it to me with your tongue cut off. On my grand momma's momma, you a dead man walking. Joe-Joe can you still hear me? On everything I love bitch..." His voice then faded to silence.

Agent Shabazz flipped Joe-Joe to an informant when they busted him on I-55 trafficking some kilos of cocaine and weapons out of state.

Joe-Joe originally gave up the E.S.B. but it didn't carry much weight because even though Agent Shabazz was familiar with them individually, he had no real knowledge of them as the E.S.B. on a larger scale. The information he received on them from Joe-Joe was just enough to open up an investigation on them. Joe-Joe then gave up Kevo who the Feds had been trying to convict for many years. Kevo out-smarted them and beat every case they brought against him.

Agent Shabazz was worried because he knew for a fact that Kevo was indeed a millionaire who could more than afford to hire the lawyers and the streets to carry out his threats. He refused to let Kevo slither out of this one, so he arranged to let Joe-Joe hide out in

Minnesota under federal protective custody until he testified.

***

After picking up a package from the Old lady, Big Face and Fats came walking in the living room of the condo where Teno and Kareem was watching the W.G.N. Nine O'clock News. Once the big flat screen TV attracted their eyes' attention, it showed Kevo running down the middle of 95th Street shooting at Joe-Joe. Then they saw Kevo taken into custody by the Feds; out of surprise and disbelief, their mouths dropped.

Big Face yelled, "Naw, naw, what the fuck? This can't be happening. They just popped our man off."

Fats said, "I told you something wasn't right about him getting out so fast."

Then Teno asked, "Who we gone fuck with now? Ain't nobody else gone hit us like dude do."

Big Face answered, "I don't know Teno... I don't know."

The following day as the E.S.B. laid low at Big Face's condo, the phone rang. Keshia answered to hear Kevo on the line from the Federal Dirksen Building downtown. She yelled, "Big Face! Aye ya'll, Kevo wife got him on three-way."

Big Face grabbed the phone and said, "What it is my dude? I saw that shit on the news."

Kevo replied, "Yeah Homie, they trying to use that fucking rat to trick a fat cat in a cage, but you know what it is. But dig, have your little brother roll with my wife and sister when they come holla and he gone give ya'll the business. Also give my wifey something to give to me to calm my nerves. You feel me?... And a ringer, you hear me?... But other than that I got you homie."

Big Face responded, "Whatever you need, we got you."

Kevo responded, "Alright then, I'll holla, love homie."

He responded back, "Keep your head up. Love."

Once they hung up, they got to packaging up some cush weed and a cell phone for Kevo's wife and Kareem to smuggle in to him. When Kareem left to visit Kevo, they waited impatiently for him to come back. When he finally made it back, Fats asked, "What was he talking about?"

He said, "After he made me promise we'll murk Joe-Joe, his wife gave me the keys to a white Cherokee truck. He says he left it parked on the side street of his gas station with a package in it for us. He says we can have it for half price which is three hundred thousand. We get to keep the truck plus he gone plug us with the connect. All we got to do is make sure at the end of the day we body bag one dude. You know we gone do Joe-Joe ass anyway, so that's nothing. He say give his wife one hundred thousand for his lawyer and he gone send us to his connect to give him that two hundred thousand he owe him so we can pick up where he left off at."

Big Face's eyes got wide as he said, "Good... good... good...consider it done baby... consider it done."

Once Kevo arranged for the E.S.B. to meet with the Mexican

Mafia, they found themselves in Olympia Fields, Illinois pulling their Tahoe truck up to a gate with armed guards. The guards requested they show identification, state their business, who they came to see, and asked if they had an appointment?

Big Face told them, "We got an appointment with Santana."

One of the guards made a call to verify. Once confirmed, the guards searched them and their vehicle before opening the gate allowing them to enter.

As they drove through the gate, Fats said, "What the fuck was that? Airport security? They was a little too rough with me. I feel violated."

Just then, a soccer ball came bouncing off the front windshield from a group of Mexicans playing what they call the real football on the giant front lawn. When they made it to the big lavish estate and walked towards the front door, they saw some black people doing lawn care and other odd jobs.

Teno asked, "What's wrong with this picture? Aren't they supposed to be the ones doing all the odd jobs we won't for cheap? And, don't they got labor laws for this type of shit?"

Fats then told him,""Shut the fuck up and ring the bell."

The large doors were opened by a grey head old Mexican lady who spoke Spanish as she led them through the house to the back yard where a group of Mexican men were lounging.

As they approached the group Big Face said, "Kay paso, amigo's. We Kevo's amigos, we here to see Santana, you comprenda?"

An old grey hair Mexican man wearing an expensive tailor-made suit, stood up and stared at him for a few moments with a plain face, then he turned to his buddies and said, "Ohites lo que este pinche idiota dijo?" Which translated means, 'Did you hear what this fucking idiot said?'

As the Mexican men broke out into laughter, he looked back at the E.S.B. who, out of ignorance, started laughing too. Then, Santanna told them, "Aye Bro, look around, do you fucking think that I got rich from only speaking Spanish? When you speak to me, we speak the universal language only and that's money: Dollars, Denaros, Pesos, and Frances. Now do you comprendé?"

Big Face replied, "Alright man, whatever, but look I got this bag of money for you so can we talk or what?"

Santanna said, "Now you speaking my language. Please come sit with us."

The E.S.B. came and sat at the large patio table with Santanna and two other men while three other men stood around the table on security.

Next, the old lady who answered the door, brought out plates of food for everyone with pig's feet, corn, and jalapeno peppers.

"I'm a Muslim, I don't eat pork," Kareem said.

"I don't eat pork either," Teno said.

Santanna told them, "You see this sweet old lady here, this is my mother. She'll be disrespected if you don't eat her food. Now, if she's disrespected, I too am disrespected."

Kareem and Teno then took a bite of the food, chewing it with unpleasant looks on their faces.

Santanna next stated, "if you got something for me, give it to me."

Kareem handed him a bag with two hundred-thousand dollars in it.

As Santanna counted the money he said, "So, you all are Kevo's business partners. He tells me you all will be continuing business as usual until he returns. I love Kevo dearly. He is like a son to me." Then, he sat the money on the table, leaned back in his seat and continued, "Gentlemen, we will be continuing the same schedule and routine as if Kevo never left. Every month, I expect a million and a half waiting for me when my men deliver the truck full of goodies. Kevo usually had the other million for me two weeks later. Now Kevo just received his truck full of goodies a week ago, and with the money you just gave me, it cleared his tab for that two and a half million. So, you got three weeks for your next shipment and to have my mill and a half with no if, ands, or buts, plus a two-week deadline to have my other million. Now, if you all can't fill my Kevo shoes, we can't do business. So gentlemen, can you all handle that?"

The E.S.B. all looked at each other with odd faces as Big Face said, "Yeah, we can handle that."

Just then, a helicopter flew overhead and landed in the yard as Santana informed them, "Gentlemen, I must rush off to my home in California, but you all are welcome to stay and enjoy yourselves for a while. My partners will take good care of you all. I'll see you fellas in three weeks."

As the men watched him fly away Kareem and Teno threw the pork into some bushes near by. They then all stood up to shake everyone's hand before leaving.

During the ride home, Kareem gripped the steering wheel and asked Fats, "I thought it was in Legions' law ya'll couldn't eat pork, and why you ain't speak up with us?"

He replied, "I don't give a fuck what our law say, I do what the fuck I want."

Then Teno said, "Ya'll need to be asking Big Face how we gone come up with that two and a half mill, because all together, I don't think we can come up with no more than five hundred thousand; maybe a million if we lucky. So just to make the million and a half, we short, let alone with a three-week deadline. Big Face, we ain't Kevo. He owns half his hood plus a few million dollar homes in the suburbs. We not moving it like he was. How we gone fill his shoes? We Just starting to see some real money so you know ain't none of us got shit stacked, cause we all too busy tricking off on cars, clothes, and hoes."

Fat's replied, "Them numbers are too big for us, plus I ain't got shit but fifty thousand stacked but fuck em', I ain't got a problem with going to war with a Mexican cartel, but we did pick a war we can't win," Big Face responded. "Yea, I stepped on the edge of the ledge, but trust me I got a plan to get that money on time."

The rest of the way home, they rode in deep thought as they rotated a blunt listening to a Mobb Deep song, "I'm going all out, with big guns and sharp knives, revolvers cause automatics jam at the wrong time..."

Narrator, Lucifer

Got my feets wet; wire tapped; D.O.C. collect calls; Cartel Mafia; Big Brothers watching ya'll; Underground; Pipeline; Dopeline; Cokelines; On the grind; Slanging dimes; Fuck indictments; I ain't doing no time; Stool pigeons; Dirty rats; Bugs bugging in my traps; Blood money; It ain't funny; Mixing work; We getting money; Trust none; Suspect all; The Feds in town; So we put em' under the ground; Bond money; Western unions; Lawyer fees; The squads free; Back down; And we gone clown; Until that last siren and chopper sound! Them just some bars to let you know how Lucifer G. feel before signing out holla!

Chapter 6

A black conversion Van trailed by a black Suburban truck rode bumper-to-bumper as they hit the freeway and crossed the Indiana border with sounds from their Memphis speakers playing a 2 Pac song, My Ambitions as a rider, "I won't deny it, I'm a straight rider, you don't wanta fuck with me, I got the police busting at me, but they can't do nothing to a G."

Inside the Van, encamped with a thick cloud of weed smoke, seven men with blood-shot eyes as if possessed by demons, pulled their ski masks down, put their hoodies on, checked their Teflon vest, then locked and loaded their assault weapons as they reached their destination. The time read 11:45P.M. when the men in the Van, plus five more in the truck, jumped out of their S.U.V.s aiming A.K's and A.R. 15's at three men who stood in front of an Indiana heroin drug spot that was known to make over $100,000 a night.

Before four other men inside the drug house, who at the time were occupied playing a John Madden Playstation game, could figure out what was going on, the front and back doors were being kicked in with choppers shoved in their faces all the while they still held the game controllers in their hands.

The three men out front, along with the four men inside, were duck-taped, hog tied, and laid on the living room floor. One of the masked men asked, "Who knows where the shit at?"

One of the men on the floor began to mumble so one of the captors snatched the duck tape off his mouth allowing him to say, "Go into the fucking bathroom and pull the floor board up, everything you jerks looking for is right there, get it and get the fuck up out of here."

One of the masked men went into the bathroom and began tearing up the floor boards. He had torn up over half of the boards before he found thirty bundles of 100, $10 jabs of dope, over 100 grams of heroin, and a little over $30,000 in cash.

Suddenly one of the lookout men came rushing in. "Ya'll speed this shit up. We got a dope line forming out there causing a traffic jam and drawing attention. They all asking who working that 'D', we need to go before they start suspecting something."

One of the mask men commanded another, "Blindfold the hostages and take them in the kitchen."

When they were all placed in the kitchen, one of the masked men pulled off his mask revealing the identity of Big Face as he said, "Ya'll grab them jabs and start serving them lines. Tiny Fou, you grab dude who told us where that shit was and take him in the bedroom. The rest of ya'll, tear this bitch up till ya'll find the real stash. Me and Tiny Fou gon make this bitch tell us where the rest at cause he gave us that little shit too fast for that to be it."

Tino, with the four recruits they brought to aid them in the robbery, went outside to secure and serve the line of dope fiends while Kareem and another guy remained outside on look out.

Big Face and Tiny Fou began to interrogate and torture K.D. who owned the dope house. After they questioned and beat K.D. for a while and he still wouldn't talk, Big Face poked a hot metal coat hanger in his eye, while demanding he give them the rest of the dope and money.

K.D. just looked at him with the other eye, laughed, and said, "Aye man, I just gave you dumb niggas everything, now you bitches either kill me or get ya'll bum ass out cause ain't shit else for ya'll clown-ass niggas to take.

Frustrated from his response, Big Face stormed out the room. He thought the take would be at least double of what they already came up on. Now he was convinced that this was all he had. As he stood in the living room area smoking a Newport cigarette, he looked over to the kitchen and seen one of the guys they brought with them watching over the hostages with an S.K. He watched Herby tear a wall down searching it as he thought to himself, Herby told me he been watching K.D. for over two months. He begged me to hit this stang with him. He told me any given day dude could be took for a key of heroin plus $100,000 or better. I may be desperate for money right now but I ain't like these dumb niggas today who see a nigga riding slick, think he got something, and go get him not knowing for sure if it's there or how much. We stalk our prey until we, and I know for sure. Herby got us on a thirsty lick.

Now, as he walked towards Herby to tell him to get everybody so we can go, he heard K.D. yell out an unusual sound. When Fats, Herby, and Big Face rushed into the room, they seen Tiny Fou who was sweating heavily pull up his pants real fast and begen to fix his belt buckle; his zipper remained unzipped.

They looked at K.D. who was laying naked curled up in a corner shaking, sitting in a small puddle of blood as if it was too hot to sit. K.D. had some white stuff dripping off his face. Hysterically, he said, "Please kill me, ya'll got to kill me now, I already told him where everything was at, now ya'll got to shoot me. Look, go into the fucking closet and tear the ceiling down, it's a key and a half of dope plus $80,000 up there. I gave ya'll everything now just don't leave me like this... Fucking shoot me now!"

Fats went over to the closet and looked inside. He tore the ceiling down, and sure enough, he found a backpack bag with the dope and money in it as K.D. had said.

As K.D. begged Big Face to kill him, they all left the room. Big Face thought, I came to rob not kill, unless I had to. This wasn't part of the plan. I got what I came for so there's no need to kill him. But as he stared at K.D. and imagined what horrific acts could of took place in the 15 minute time span he wasn't in the room, he came to the conclusion, I got what I wanted I can at least give him what he wants. He walked over to K.D., aimed his pistol at his head, and watched him lay his forehead on the barrel of his gun, as he began to say a prayer. When he was finished praying and said, "Amen," Big Face pulled the trigger and watched his brains splatter on the wall as his body fell to the floor before he walked out the room.

Outside, Teno with four of the guys, had just finished serving the dope fiends and clearing the block when they heard the shot. They let the other hostages live, leaving them in the kitchen as they evacuated, fleeing in their S.U.V's to another destination.

On their way to another location, the men inside the van remained quiet out of disbelief, stuck in thought. They were all stunned from what they could only imagine had taken place in the room with Tiny Fou and K.D.

The silence in the van was suddenly interrupted with laughter when Fats imitated a Katt Williams scene, "I'm a boy, God damn it."

The E.S.B had brought eight stick-up men with them from out east. These were guys they grew up with and knew. Herby was one of those guys they recruited. He was Big Face's childhood friend who used to live in the Manor. He was also a Goblin.

Herby was a cut-throat stick up man who robbed everybody including his own momma.

Big Face, for some unknown reason, was the only one he never crossed, so they remained friends. The streets eventually put a price on Herby's head so he relocated to Indiana where he continued his mayhem. Whenever he stalked big game, that would be a big pay day. He would contact Big Face to see if he wanted in on the stang.

Big Face knew Herby would get him killed so he always refused but, with him needing cash to pay the Mexican Mafia, he was all in on this one.

The eighth man was Tiny Fou. He was a guy who stayed in jail most of his life. It was a rumor that while in prison all the guys that didn't pay back his two-for-one-loans on time, would get knocked out and fucked by him. He was indeed a true jail bird nigga who Fats originally met in juvenile detention.

Tiny Fou was in the Four Knives gang and Fats was in the

Legions. They were in alliance with each other which made it easy for them to click up to gangbang and rob guys in juvenile detention. Later, they met back up when they began their freshman year at Corliss High school, which was around the corner from where Tiny Fou lived.

The first week of school, Tiny Fou got arrested for murdering another student in front of the school. He did a few years before beating it on appeal. He'd only been out thirteen months since then and was now with his homie Fats doing what he loved to do, take shit.

Tiny Fou leaned up to the driver giving him directions to his girlfriend Naomi's house. He'd been fucking her for nine months now. She was the cutest thing you ever seen. A Meagan Goode look alike with a baby voice. She was their next victim. Tiny Fou had been plotting on his bitch since the first day he met her. Now, as they left Indiana going back to Chicago at two A.M., the squad was on their way to capture and rob more prey.

As they slowly pulled up to a four story building that held eight condos, Tiny Fou accompanied by another guy, went to the front door while Tino, who was accompanied by four more guys, went around to the back. Tiny Fou pressed Naomi's buzzer until she woke up.

"Who is it?"

Tiny Fou answered, "Naomi, it's me baby, Johnathen Baker. I know it's late, and I'm sorry for waking you up, but it's important baby. I promise I'll make it up to you, Boo."

When Tiny Fou got out the joint for that murder thirteen months ago he stole the identity of Johnathen Baker and got several credit cards to pay for his new lavish life style. Now as Naomi buzzed the door open, little did she know the man that she thought was Johnathen was a lie.

When they made it upstairs to the top floor and entered her condo, she asked, "Baby, who you bringing into my house this early?"

As he looked around he asked, "Naomi, who you got in here with you?"

"Nobody fool, just me and my son Daniel," she said.

Tiny Fou swung a mean right jab and knocked her out as his accomplice closed the door then went to the back door to let the others in.

Naomi was a manager at a bank on 95th and Oak Park; she was the one who had the keys to open up the Bank every morning. Now, as he held ice on her pretty face, she woke up witnessing his face with a house full of masked men who were all armed. She screamed, "Where's Daniel? What ya'll do with my son?"

He said, "Sssshhh... Daniel's fine baby, he's still in his room sleeping. It's some men in there babysitting him, so if you don't do what they say, they gone make sure he don't wake up, and then put you to sleep with him. So, just do what you are told, and when it's over, they'll let you and your son go to live happily ever after, O.K. baby." Then kissed her on the cheek as tears ran down her pretty face. He next told her, "Look baby, these men going to stay here and babysit Daniel... sssshhhh don't speak, they not gon touch him, he's safe. They just gon watch him to make sure you do what you are told. Now, while they watch him, you gon go with us to the bank so you can open it up for us and let us into the vault. Once we get what we want, we gone leave you at work, then I'll call Daniel's babysitters to let them know they can leave. Then, you can call the police and say anything you want except for anything about me, cause if anything happen to me, them masked men will make sure cute little Daniel mysteriously disappears, only to return to you in a box chopped up in a million pieces. So, be a team player baby, and get dressed." Tiny Fou had no intentions of harming Daniel, but full intentions of killing his pretty little momma afterwards.

Tiny Fou escorted Naomi to the truck where they proceeded to the location of the Bank in both S.U.Vs. It was 5:42 A.M. when they pulled into the bank's parking lot.

Naomi usually arrives at six A.M. to let the employees in to set up their stations which is prior to the doors opening for customers at seven A.M.

They have less than eighteen minutes before employees and security arrives. They plan to be in and out in ten minutes leaving Naomi's brains scattered all over the vault while they walked out with bags full of money.

Tiny Fou put a Sarah Palen mask over his head then pulled Naomi out of the truck. He walked her to the bank's front door while the two accomplices with him, got out the truck to serve as look-outs.

In the van next to them, Big Face put a president Barak Obama mask on his head; Fats a Ronald Regan mask; and Herby, a George Bush mask before exiting the van to follow behind them. Kareem drove the van around on look-out.

Once she unlocked the door, all five of them where inside and walking towards the vault ready for her to open it.

She realized and explained, "Wait...I can't open it until 6:45 A.M. It's on a timer. There's nothing I can do to get it open until then."

Tiny Fou, whose identity was Sarah Palen, looked at Obama and said, "What now, commander in chief?"

Obama replied, "I guess it's time for change... We gon be here to greet the employees."

Sarah Palan responded, "You bet cha!"

Naomi looked at all their mask like a little frightened kid and began to cry.

Next, the men set up to greet the employees. Sarah Palen wrapped a scarf around his neck to make it seem more natural as he stood at the door with Naomi to watch over her as she let the employees inside.

Obama stood beside the door with a S.K. to greet them as they entered while Regan escorted them to an office where Bush would lay them on the floor and watch over them with an A.K.

Now, as the clock ticked, Obama told Naomi to smile while they held their positions waiting on the first employee to report in for work.

Meanwhile, a guy name James who lived in Naomi's building on the first floor, went up to her condo to get her for their date. James and Naomi had been sneaking around on Johnathen for a few months. The day before, Naomi had told James she had an off day tomorrow and requested he come get her at six A.M. so she could take her son to his grandmother's house. Afterwards, he could sex her body for the whole day with no interruptions.

It was 6:05 and James knocked on her door with nasty thoughts of what they was gone do to each other.

When Teno heard the knocks at the door, he looked through the peek hole and seen a clean-cut, white dude. He commanded one of the men to go wake up Daniel and bring him to the door.

The man woke Daniel up and brought him out.

Daniel asked, "Where's my Mommy?"

Teno told him, "Mommy will be back real soon. She had to go to work. We're your uncles. We watching you until she gets back. Now Daniel, I need you to answer the door and tell that man, your Mommy's at work and your uncle 'D' is busy so he should come back later."

After he said, "Alright," Teno hid behind the door and opened it up just enough for him to see Daniel.

James seen Daniel was still in his Sponge Bob P.J's and asked, "Where is your mother?"

"She at work and uncle 'D' said he's busy come back later." Daniel said.

Teno slammed the door close and watched the white man leave through the peek hole.

James knew today was her off day and suspected something was seriously wrong. He used to tell Naomi all the time that she should leave Johnathen for him because he didn't deserve a woman like her. He also used to tell her that if he ever hit her, to let him know. He told her that because he sensed some domestic violence in their relationship. Now, as James headed back to his condo, in his mind he believed Johnathen was up there beating on her, because he knew for a fact she wasn't at work today. In addition, she would never allow her son to answer the door unless something was seriously wrong.

James grabbed his phone to call the police, reporting a woman being beaten to death by a jealous boyfriend in front of her son.

Back upstairs, Daniel continued to yell and cry until his request for some Captain Crunch Berry cereal was met. Teno knew he had to keep the little boy quiet to keep from drawing attention from the neighbors. So instead of using force, he told Daniel, "If you keep quiet like a good little boy, your uncle 'D' will go to the store and get you that box of cereal."

The boy kept quiet so he went out, on foot, to the nearest store. By the time he made it to the corner, a line of marked and unmarked police cars flew pass him swarming Naomi's building.

The squad of officers kicked Naomi's door down catching one man raising a shotgun pump up, but they shot him down before he could pull the trigger. Two other men, who was caught off guard, sitting on the couch surrendered by dropping their guns as they raised their hands in the air.

Then, they began searching all the rooms and kicked open the door to Daniel's room. They saw a man holding a gun to a little boy's head yelling, "Back the fuck up! Back the fuck up!"

As officers stood in a standoff with guns drawn at the man, one decided to take a shot that went right between the gunman's eyes, causing him to fall and drop the gun without harming the boy.

Once Teno heard the shots from a block away, he took the first car he saw by breaking the window, pulling the steering wheel collar, and finally pulling the pin until the engine rammed up. Then, he casually fled the scene as his heart beat fast.

***

At 6:01 A.M. a white, middle-aged woman name Margret Jackson pulled into the bank's parking lot, singing along to her favorite song by Willow Smith, "I whip my hair back and forth." Margret was also a manager at the bank who had the keys to open up on Naomi's days off. As she sat in her car singing and dancing to her favorite song, she seen Betty, a middle-aged, black woman who was an employee enter the bank.

She thought to herself, how did she get in? Her intuition told her to stay in the car for a few minutes, that's when she saw Frank, a fat, white guy who was the bank's security officer walk into the bank. For fourteen years straight, Frank always went inside to punch his time card and then came right out to circle the bank's perimeter before heading next door to the donut shop. But today, when he didn't come out, she waited five minutes then called the police on her cell phone stating, "Hi, I'm the manager at First National Bank and I'm the one who opens up. But for some reason, it was already open and there are a lot of unusual activities taking place. Would you please send someone over?"

The dispatcher asked her, "Where are you?"

She answered, "In the parking lot."

The dispatcher told her, "Stay put. We're sending some squad cars now to check it out."

Meanwhile, in the bank employees continued to arrive. A young, white employee name Kelly walked in with a smile on her face that instantly turned to a face of fear when she noticed Naomi standing with Sarah Palen, who had an assault weapon held on her. Then she saw Obama and Regan pointing their weapons at her and directing her to an office where Bush instructed her to lay on the floor with the rest of the employees.

When the clock in the bank read 6:46 A.M. Obama told Naomi, "Alright Missy, time to open up that vault."

When the vault doors opened up, Sarah Palen pushed Naomi down on the floor of the vault and told her, "Lay down and don't move."

Obama and Sarah Palen, like fat happy kids in a candy store, each pulled out two large bags and began to stuff them with money. Suddenly, on their two-way radio, they heard Kareem yelling, "Get the fuck out now! 5.0's on the way! Get the fuck out! 5.0's on their fucking way!"

The four bags were only half full when they grabbed them to flee the bank. Before leaving the vault, Sarah Palen turned around and shot Naomi in the back while she lay on the floor. Then they ran towards the front door throwing a bag of money at Bush and Regan.

When all four made it out the front door, they were greeted by two squad cars who they quickly engaged them in a gun fight. As the squad cars received a round of bullets, the officers climbed out to the other side of the car to take cover before returning shots.

Two of the men who set up in the parking lot as look-outs came out of nowhere spraying the officers with bullets that left their dead bodies bleeding all over their squad cars. A line of back-up ringing their sirens pulled in the bank's lot as the two look-out men fled in one direction while the other four men with the bags of money in another.

As Tiny Fou cut into an alley trailing behind Big Face, Fats, and Herby, a squad car pulled up with two SWAT officers fully suited in armor jumped out. Tiny Fou turned around; spraying bullets, he hit one in the neck killing him instantly.

The other SWAT officer shot him continuously until his body danced and fell while the wind blew some money in the shot up bag he dropped.

Once the look-outs ran, some of the squad cars followed in hot pursuit which caused them to flee in opposite directions.

When they got a good distance away, one of the men hid under a two flat home porch while the other man ran in an alley and jumped inside a large commercial trash bin.

Cop cars surrounded the trash bin when they spotted the lid closing. One of the officers threw a pepper spray bomb into the bin to draw him out.

When the gunman stuck his gun out the bin to bust a few shots, the officers stuck their guns inside to return fire until he was dead.

As Big Face, Herby, and Fats ran down a residential street, they spotted one of their guys who was on look-out wave them over to where he was hiding under a porch. Once under the porch, they realized they couldn't continue to run with the large bags of money. They decided to stuff as much money as possible on themselves.

They were only able to stuff a half of bag on them so they decided to hide the bags under the porch and come back for them later.

After they spotted Kareem riding past in the van, all four men chased behind, waving, and screaming until they seen the brake lights come on and the van stopped.

Just as the van side doors slid open and Fats and Herby jumped inside, a squad car with two officers rolled up shooting, and killing their look-out man as he tried to jump into the van.

Big Face sprayed shots recklessly killing both officers as he dived into the van just as Kareem pulled off.

Big Face, Fats, Kareem, and Herby all met back up with Teno at the safe house. After giving an account of what happen to all their men, a disappointing $608,000 was totaled up from what all three men escaped with.

Much later at nine P.M., a W.G.N. News reporter reported, "Early this morning, a woman who was the manager at First National Bank home was invaded by her boyfriend and several other men, who held her five year old son hostage while they took her to open the bank. The five year old was safely retrieved by officers while two kidnappers were killed and two arrested. The woman was shot in the back during the robbery and is now in the hospital recovering from her wound. Three bank robbers were killed by officers while a few unidentified assailants escaped. The police retrieved most of the eight million stolen, finding one bag of money on a man they killed in an alley and three more bags of money under a porch of a two flat home. This incident left five officers dead with several injured."

The bank heist was a failure. They set out on a twenty- four hour robbing spree and their mission wasn't complete yet. The lost of their men would have made the average crew fall back but this gave them motivation to proceed. Now, as the cush smoke filled their lungs, they all agreed they would continue on because they heard the voices of their dead homies telling them, "Get money niggas, our blood ain't shed in vain, stang em' for us, so our spirits will live on hitting licks."

Hearing these voices is what was supposed to have pushed them, but deep down if they did or didn't, they knew the real reason was because they had to make a quota.

The E.S.B., along with Herby, then strategized their next heist. Kevo and Mann were Chicago's biggest drug lords. They were your suppliers, supplier who had the whole city on lock. Now with Kevo in the Fed joint, Mann, who sold heavy weight in any kind of drug you could think of, now had the city on lock all by herself. This Mrs. Dope lady was the E.S.B's next victim.

When they arrived at her house, no one was there so Big Face and Herby hid in the bushes in front of her house while Fats and Teno hid around back; Kareem laid low in the van. Not long after, Kareem on the two-way informed them, "Dinners coming."

That's when the four men with ski-masks on locked and loaded their weapons. Mann's purple Bently G.T. pulled in the driveway beating out the speakers a Yo Gotti song, "Look in the Mirror," "I became a millionaire and I was selling dope."

Before getting out the car, Mann's girlfriend Soshia sat up in the passenger seat to put on her lipstick.

Soshia was a pretty, young thang who resembled Diamond, an ex Crime Mob rapper.

Now, as Soshia put the key in the door, Mann squeezed on her soft ass, gripping it with passion, as she stood behind her, kissing her on the back of her neck. When Soshia opened the door, Big Face and Herby jumped out the bushes, masked up with assault weapons in hand, they pushed them into the house.

Once inside the house, Big Face searched them and took a Tec nine from Mann before sitting them on the couch while Herby went to the back to let the others in.

Big Face, whose identity was hidden behind a mask, held an S.K. to Mann's face while he said, "You got 60 seconds to turn over all the fucking money and dope. I know you got over a milly in here, so if you even think of short changing me, your face gonna be all over your pretty bitch."

Mann responded, "I don't keep that type of cash just lying around here like that."

The whole time while this was going on, Soshia was staring at Teno, whose identity was also hidden behind a mask.

When Teno opened his mouth to say, "Bitch, well you better tell us where it is laying around like that then."

Recognizing his voice, Soshia excited said, "Teno!... That's you? Why you doing this to us? You punk, sissy-ass nigga, leave us alone."

A little over a year ago when Teno was broke, him and Soshia was a couple. When she got pregnant, she left him for a major hustler who used to spoil her. Even when her baby boy was born looking just like Teno, she still proclaimed it wasn't his, but instead, her new boyfriend's son, who she loved dearly until he went to jail. Then, became Mann's bitch.

Mann said, "Big Face, I knew that sounded like you. Take that fucking mask off. Soshia, them two other niggas is Kareem and Fats. I knew once Kevo left, ya'll was gone come holla at me, but not like this. Shit... I know ya'll tired of being broke, just be easy. I'll put ya'll on. But first, let me guess this was Big Face's idea? Ain't nobody gon put ya'll on with this over aggressive games. Nigga, put them toy guns down so we can talk business."

Then, Soshia said, "Ya'll know ya'll ain't gone shoot nothing."

They all took their mask off while Big Face told them, "Ya'll silly hoes so smart; ya'll dumb cause now we get to kill ya'll dumb ass's unless the price is right, so what the fuck is it gonna be, ya'll wanna live or die?"

Mann responded, "Look homie, I'm trying to give you nikkle-and-dime ass niggas a job cause gangsters respect gangstas shit. But, if ya'll keep this dumb shit up, I'ma take all ya'll bitches and put them hoes on You-tube with me eating their pussies, tongue kissing them, and fucking them with my strap-on. So, what the fuck it's gonna be? A job or You-Tube?"

Big Face told Herby and Teno to search the house while he tied their hands and feet up. Then, he hit Soshia in the mouth and ripped her skimmpy little dress off, leaving her on the couch with just her bra on. He told her, "I love a bitch who don't wear panties." Next, he ripped her bra off revealing her pretty titties, he squeezed them, stuck his finger in her pussy and said, "You think your he-she lover will get mad if I fuck you in front of her?"

Mann then said, "Nigga your dick ain't big enough. You ain't gone do shit but get her hot and ready for me."

Big Face furiously began to beat Mann in the face until she fell to the ground laughing.

With her face bloody, Mann said, "You must be mad my dick bigger than yours."

Soshia was crying and let out a painful moan as Fats stuck the barrel of an A.K. inside her pussy and said, "Look at this. You think this funny? Your bitch ain't worth that little money huh?" Then, he pulled the barrel out of her until it was between her legs by her upper thigh and then, he shot her.

She laid on the couch with her arms and legs tied up pleading, "Please don't kill me. Mann... baby... please give them what they want so they can go."

Mann said nothing and turned her head away to stare at the floor.

Big Face then grabbed her by her braids and drug her into a side bedroom where you could see in it from the couch. He told her, "You dike-ass bitch, you really think you a man huh? Well, I'm about to show you, you a bitch and what your pussy really made for." He tied her hands to the bed. She laid on her back as he tore her clothes off. All along Mann continued to ram on, "I ain't giving you niggas shit! Shoot me nigga!"

Big Face pulled his erected dick out, put her legs over his shoulders, and forced his dick inside her tight dry pussy.

Mann squeezed her eyes shut and screamed, "Ah ah ah ah ahwww."

He told her, "Bitch, you really is a virgin, huh. Well, now you can tell everybody that, that big dick gangsta who took your virginity popped your cherry."

In a painful voice, she replied, "Ah ah ahww... I was just waiting on a nigga like you who was cuter than my bitch to be my first. Now kiss me while you give me that dick."

Fats, who was standing by the couch looking in, started laughing. Big Face looked up at him and asked, "You want some of this?"

He said, "Hell naw, I'm straight."

Mann continued to scream in pain as he pounded as hard as he could until she came and screamed out, "Oh oh oh oh sh sh shiiit! I just had my first fucking orgasm."

"Thank you baby, I'm glad you came," she said as he pulled his pants up and stormed out the room frustrated thinking to himself, I refuse to let this be a failed mission. He went to sit on the couch with Soshia, who was bleeding then looked into the room at Mann.

She was yelling, "What, we can t cuddle now? You just gone hit it and leave, huh? You my baby daddy now. I'ma tell your baby mama I'm pregnant by you."

Fats stood there trying to hold his laughter in as she continued to taunt him saying, "Yeah, your bitch Keshia thick. After I make her sit that big booty on my face, I m gonna get the biggest dildo I can find and fuck the shit out of her like you just did me. Your little dick ain't gone fit in her after I bust her pussy open and fuck her until she bleed. Then I'ma fuck her in that big ass she got until she get hemorrhoids and got to tuck her asshole back in. Aye Big Face, your pretty little daughter Alivia, I'm gonna do her the same way except I'm gonna make her a dike like me afterwards, so nigga is we getting married or what?"

Fats said, "Kill that bitch before I do."

Big Face jumped up with a face filled with rage as he went into the room and said, "Alright, you wanna be a man... I'ma show you what happens to men who got bitch in them."

He finally figured out how to get through to her when Tiny Fou's spirit came to life to reveal to him the secret tactic. He flipped Mann over to doggy-style position then stripped her butt naked. Next, he shoved his rock hard dick up her ass. Tearing through her anus, he pounded vigorously and rapidly as her ass cheeks loudly clapped against his body.

She yelled from the top of her lungs from the violent pain. She pleaded and begged him to stop, telling him where three million was hidden in the house plus where all the drugs was at.

But, Big Face possessed by anger and revenge for the threats she made towards his family, was in a zone where he wasn't aware of, or heard anything, in his surroundings. Even if he did hear her, he would have continued to tear through the flesh of her anus, feeling numb to the pain he was enduring himself.

Fats ran upstairs to the attic finding an armory of guns and a safe. He could still hear her yelling the combination to the safe as he opened it up. Packing up all the money and calling Teno to gather up all the guns. He called Herby to follow him to the garage where they grabbed sledge hammers to break up the concrete floor.

The whole back half of the floor appeared to be concrete, but was only a wooden floor board that was easily busted up revealing a six foot by six foot square hole in the ground that was filled with pounds of weed, coke, and heroin. Fats and Herby loaded everything into a Range Rover that was parked in the garage.

When they finished, they went back inside the house. Big Face was still naked, fucking Mann up the ass while she stared at the wall chanting in an unknown language, just laying there as if she was numb to the pain. Teno shot Soshia in the head while Fats pulled Big Face off Mann.

Herby poured gasoline all over Mann as she lay in doggy-style position as if nothing changed.

They put their masks back on, except Big Face who was still stuck in zombie mode.

Fats, who was frustrated, wanted to shoot him because now he was jeopardizing their life and freedom by being careless. Instead, he held it in and put a mask over Big Face's head. Then, he directed Herby to escort him out the back into the Rover while him and Teno ran out front to the van with the bags of money and guns, leaving behind a house of flames.

Once back at the safe house with Big Face back in his Boss state of mind, he gathered all the money and counted up a total of $3,718,000 in cash while the rest of the guys played like little kids with the spoils from the heist, which was a shit load of weed, heroin, cocaine, and guns.

Starting out with twelve men and only making it back with five, they lost more than they came home with. But, at the end of the day, they would make their spoils compensate for their loses.

Narrator, Lucifer

Aye, check out how I feel, "I'll lie for it; make you cry for it; down to die for it; steal for it; down to kill for it; cause I live for it; bust steal for it; come back on appeal for it; wheel and deal for it; but never will I fold, bend over, bitch, kneel, or squeal for it!" Now that's what the fuck I'm talking about. Choppers plus ski-mask equals a whole lot of cash. Now, they got more than enough to pay them Mexicanos. Now, the world is about to be their's. Them East Side boys going hard in the mutha fuckin pain't for it. East Side or die... all for it! The spirit of Err, A.K.A. Lucifer G's all for it!

Chapter 7

On a Monday morning at 8:52 A.M. three young black women named Erika, Nicole, and Tammy, who shared a home at 67th and Eberhart, rushed three kids out the house into a white Cherokee truck to send them off to elementary school. When they returned home, a white delivery truck flashing its lights, with three Mexican men inside was waiting for them in the middle of the street in front of their house.

Erika got out the truck she was driving to yell, "When ya'll called this morning, I told you hot pepper, taco-eating mutha fucka's to come at ten o'clock so our kids wouldn't be here when this came. Now ya'll lucky our kids just left."

The delivery men began to carry in large boxes that on the side read Sony, RCA, and Koss.

One of the Mexican men said to another, "Que la vieja boca grande es el pelo defelteo una peluca," which when translated to English means, "Do you think that's the lady with the big mouth real hair, a weave, or a wig?"

The other Mexican man answered, "Ninguna, de ellas es un gata." Which means "Niether one, it's a cat."

When Erika seen them all laughing, she yelled, "You mutha fuckas talking about me? I bet you won't say that shit to me in English you Tabasco-smelling bastards."

Nicole then told her, "Girl, be cool, you're drawing attention."

She responded, "That's why I didn't want this shit to come to my house anyway. I can't believe I let you hoes talk me into this."

Then Tammy spoke up talking to Erika, "Bitch, you should of said no before you took that money and that truck... Yeah bitch, I thought so. Now, call Big Face and tell him these people here."

As the delivery men took in the last of the boxes, the E.S.B. pulled up with their new accomplice, Herby. While the rest of them went into the house with the women, Big Face got into the delivery truck with one of the Mexicans and gave him two and a half million in cash. He then told him, "Tell Santana I don't need no extension. That's all his money and I'll see him again in four weeks to do it again." Then he got out the truck and went in the house.

Once he stepped inside the house and saw the ripped open boxes revealing kilos of heroin and cocaine, he instructed Herby and Kareem to go secure the outside of the house while the rest of them sorted and stashed the kilos in the new safe house.

Now in this era, if you had a good solid connect the average wholesale price for cocaine was $18.5 a kilo, $10,000 for a half, and $800-$1,000 an ounce. Heroin was $75-$80,000 a kilo, and $80-$125 a gram. Cush weed was $35-$3,700 a pound and $300 an ounce. Ecstasy pills was $5 a pill and jars of 500 for $2,200.

Remember, these were dealers prices not retail.

Thanks to the E.S.B's new Mexican connect, they was getting pure cocaine for $7,000 a kilo. They would turn that into three, slanging them for $10,000 to $14,000 a bird. They gave them heroin for $25,000 a key that after hitting they slung 1,000 grams for $50,000 and $50 a gram. The heroin was so pure, dealers still had to hit it with at least a ten before putting it out on the streets.

The Nigerians fed them cush weed at $500 a pound that they turned around and slang for $2,000 a pound. They also gave them ecstasy pills at $500 for 1,000 pills. They slung single pills for $7 and jars of 500 for $1,500.

If you bought over 5,000 pills, you got each at $1.50. To top it off, just to show their appreciation, the Nigerians used to just give them prometazine and codeine. They sold ounces of lean for $10 a bottle.

Erika

The E.S.B. was well acquainted with and trusted Erika, Tammy, and Nicole only because Erika was Teno's cousin.

Teno's mother, Gloria, use to babysit her niece and Big Face when they were youngsters. Big Face looked at Erika as if she was his real cousin, which is the reason why he instilled so much trust in her.

Erika had a nine-year-old son named Derrick. She was a five foot four inches tall, 150-pound, thick, tan complexion black woman. She was deeply into the latest fads and fashion; Jimmy Cho, Gucci, Louis Vuitton, Prada, Chanel, Victoria Secret, Dior, Fendi, you name it she had it.

Every week. she had a reserved seat at the beauty shop to get her hair and nails done. What stood out about her wasn't her top of the line attire, it was her bitch attitude. She couldn't go anywhere without cussing somebody out. In her world, her pussy and ass smelt like peaches and strawberries. She was the shit and it didn't stink. She was definitely your high maintenance bitch.

When Erika was only fourteen years old, an old-school, hood-rich hustler name Dollar, who loved to trick off on young girls, got her pregnant. She was in her first year at Hyde Park high school and had to drop out. She moved in with her sugar daddy, Dollar. That's when she got addicted to shopping. This resulted from her unlimited access to her baby-daddy Dollar's dollars.

Five years ago, Dollar was found dead in the trunk of his Lexus allegedly from a drug deal gone bad. She knew where he stashed all his money in the house so she did well maintaining her lavish life style after his death, plus the house they lived in on 67th and Eberhart was owned and paid for by Dollar, and it was turned over to her.

Nicole and Tammy were her long time friends. They also had kids and needed a place to stay. Therefore, she invited them to be her housemates and to keep her company since Dollar was gone.

Because it had been five years since Dollar died, Erika was having trouble maintaining her lifestyle and couldn't even afford to replace the Lincoln Navigator that recently got stolen. Erika and her girlfriends together could barely afford to pay the bills on time.

Erika needed a loan fast so she decided to reach out to her cousin Teno and tell him her situation. She contacted him at the right time, too. Teno and Big Face decided to give her the white Cherokee truck they got from Kevo, some money to help her get on her feet, and a job they could only trust family with. Teno and Big Face knew Nicole and

Tammy as Erika's long time friends who could be trusted so they decided to put them to work also.

Tammy

Tammy was a pretty six-foot, 120-pound, light brown complexion, black female with silky. long hair, who favored the singer Aaliyah. She had a seven-year-old daughter, named Cece, by a small-time hustler name Little 'O'. Even though they had a so-called open relationship, her baby daddy, Little 'O', used to get jealous when he seen her with other guys, and that always resulted in him beating her up. Tammy always forgave him because afterwards, he took her and their daughter on a shopping spree.

Little 'O' wanted to have it where he could fuck his baby momma anytime he wanted to with no relationship involved; that's exactly how he had it.

Erika had been encouraging her to stop fucking with him completely and to hook up with her cousin Teno. Teno and Tammy were just friends and he was never about to get into a relationship with her. But, he did upgrade their relationship to fucking buddies with a strict understanding that they were just friends who fucked sometime. Little 'O' eventually found out Teno was fucking his baby momma but he dared not to intervene.

Nicole

Nicole was a five foot five inches tall, 162-pound, thick, red bone with red hair who always wore red lipstick on her full, thick lips. She was the sexiest thing you'd ever seen. She had a nine-year-old daughter named Micheal who looked like a mini her. Her baby daddy was in jail for murder with a life sentence, but she stayed dedicated to him by bringing their daughter to see him and putting money on his books.

She danced in a few bootleg rappers videos and wanted to be a choreographer one day. Nicole was also a part-time dancer at a strip-club where when she got onto the stage and moved her body, it was hypnotizing to everyone in the club, putting them in a trance.

Every time Little 'O' went to see Tammy and his daughter, his crew Tom-Tom and Mike, who liked Nicole, always went with him to see which one of them would come up and fuck her first. In every attempt they made, she would diss them with no regards.

Now that the girls were established with the E.S.B. and their house was one of their major safe houses, they decided to take over the house across the street turning it into a trap house where they had the girls selling nothing but keys out of it. Any business you did with the E.S.B., went through the girls. They played puppet master with these females to keep the heat and spotlight off themselves. These three women were basically test-dummies who would get it first, letting them know when the Feds and stick-up men were in town.

These three women enjoyed the glory, money, and fame. Bitches doing it like men riding around town flossing, competing with the male hustlers, like their thoroughness made this shit happen. Only a few knew this shit would never be, or even last, if the E.S.B. wasn't behind them. For this was a man's world where a bitch could never hold it down unless a man was behind her.

Now with all the major hustlers who feed the city being either dead, locked up, or on the run the city was open for the taking, and with no hesitation the E.S.B. took it. They flooded the city of Chicago making it rain with keys for dirt-cheap. Chicago wasn't just the city that works, it was the city that had work. Once the word got out that the dope was good and the price was right, dope boys from out of state hit the freeway to take advantage of the Chicago pipeline. The streets of Chicago was soon flooded with out of state license plates. The trap houses that use to sell dime bags now sold dope by the ounces and grams.

They secured their grip on the city by enforcing an E.S.B. or die policy. Anyone who wasn't with the E.S.B. mob was considered against them, so they boxed their rivals in and made them offers they couldn't refuse. Either join them to prosper in the fruits of the hustle or die. Few protested making it easier for them to grip the city of Chi like a vise grip, making it snow in the city during the summer and hot as hell in the winter but yet instill cold all year round, while they slanged birds to out-of-towners.

Guys who joined the E.S.B. mob received so much love from them that they were willing to cut their own momma's throats for them. The prices offered to their members only was lovely. The have-nots became the have-it-all's. Like a Getto boy's song, "If life was a game that money could buy, the rich niggas would live and the poor niggas a die."

Life had to be a game that money could buy because every member of the E.S.B. was living life, even its members in jail behind bars was living life. One E.S.B. member had an extra cell just to keep his commissary in. You had incarcerated members still paying mortgages and giving their love ones gifts fresh off the car lots. The high life was on the trading block sold by the Devil, and the E.S.B. bought it.

The growing spread of the E.S.B. mob was like a rapid wild fire that sent the reaper to those who opposed. If you were approached, you better not flag or scream nothing but E.S.B. or you died.

At a dope line in front of a house in South Chicago a man who appeared to be your average dirty dope fiend asked one of the three dealers outside, 'Ya'll E.S.B? Is this that E.S.B. work?' When one of the dealers responded, 'Fuck them E.S.B. niggas. Bitch, this our work!' The dope fiend, along with five other dope fiends, opened fire killing all three dealers outside. They then ran into the house to kill four other men. One dealer who was hiding under a bed was suddenly pulled from under the bed by two of the dope fiends.

As he begged for his life, one of them grabbed him by his dread-locks, held an ax over his head and said, 'We told you little niggas E.S.B. or die. Then gave ya'll thirty days. Today, make thirty and ya'll not E.S.B. so now ya'll getting the die part.'

Then, he swung the ax at his neck causing his body to drop while he still held onto his dreadlocks with his head dangling from it.

Later that night, a news castor interviewed a lady who looked like Keshia Cole's momma Frankie and who just so happen to be named Frankie telling them, 'I'm a recovering drug addict and I was in line telling my boyfriend, baby you need to leave this stuff alone. When ten to twenty guys just got to shooting, pow... pow.. pow.., so I ran to hid behind a car when I heard something say, 'Frankie look up.' So, I looked up at the house and could see it lighting up like a crack pipe being lit with a cotton ball and some alcohol. But anyway, what was I just talking about?... Oh yeah, I then seen twenty to thirty masked men with bazookas wearing sandals looking like the Taliban, so I prayed, God, if you let me make it home safe, I promise I won't do no more drugs.' Now I told ya'll what happened, you still gon give me that ten dollars?'

Three Englewood high school boys on their way home walked pass eight other young boys who was standing on the corner of 63rd and Halsted. One of the boys on the corner said, "You dudes be E.S.B.'?"

One of the three responded, "I'm a Devil."

One of the eight boys responded back, "I don't give a fuck about all of that. You must ain't get the news that, that shit don't matter no more. So I'ma ask you punk ass niggas one more time, do you be E.S.B. or what?"

One of the three boys then said, "Is ya'll serious cause we not out East. This the south-side plus we Devils like ya'll, fam. I'm frommm..."

But before he could finish speaking, he was hit in the jaw. The eight boys next beat and stomped the three boys until they were passed out in comas laying on the corner bleeding. Then, one of the boys took their knock-off Air-one gym shoes and fake Louis Vuitton jacket before running off yelling, "E.S.B. or die bitch!"

On 75th and Stony Island, a white Escalade truck stopped at a red light behind a chameleon-color '95 Chevy Impala. The Lamborghini doors on the Chevy went up then three armed men jumped out and ran up to the truck pointing guns and asking the men in the truck, "You niggas E.S.B.?"

The driver responded, "What you talking about? We ain't on none of that shit."

The gunmen pulled them out the truck and forced them to lay face down in the street. As the light turned green, a man in a black Benz pulled up behind the truck and yelled, "Aye, what the fuck is wrong with ya'll?"

When they seen who he was, one of the gunmen, Little Ray Ray who was a 17-year-old E.S.B. member said to his homie, "That's one of the Dons... Teno." Then he yelled back to Teno, "They say they not E.S.B. so we about to do they ass."

Teno got out his car, walked up and seen that the three men on the ground was Tom Tom, Mike, and Little 'O', he told Little Ray Ray, "Naw, I know them. Ya'll stand the fuck down and get them the fuck up off the ground. Ya'll went mad. Ya'll was gone really do em' in the middle of traffic in front of everybody? Ya'll true E.S.B. soldiers for real. Don't trip, I got some work for ya'll to do. But hurry up and get the fuck up out of here before the police come."

He looked at Little 'O', who had the fear of God in his face and told him, "Ya'll owe me. Just make sure ya'll get ya'll work from me for now on and we even. Plus, ya'll won't have to worry about shit like this no more." He gave Little 'O' his number before driving off.

Local gang chiefs was given the option to, within 24 hours, either bring their whole membership to join the E.S.B. mob with a guarantee of keeping their authority over their gang under E.S.B. authority, or they all died.

One gang chief refused to flip his gang, so he prepared his men for an all out war against the E.S.B. mob. Many of his members feared for their lives because they had been hearing and seeing all around town the brutal take down, takeover tactics used by them to take over territories with their hood next on the hit list.

Members who seen benefits of their gang joining, formed a secret revolt. At a gang meeting, held in a local park, to discuss their war strategy against the E.S.B. mob, some revolts pulled out baby Uzies and Mac 10's on all who wasn't rebels. One shot their gang chief in the head.

One of the rebels said, "I'm stepping up to represent us in branching with the E.S.B. mob, so we can come up and stay in control of our neighborhood. If we don't, we gonna be broke, most of us gone die, and some E.S.B. niggas gone move in and get rich. So, we gon get money and still hold our land down. Now, whoever ain't with us, let me know."

After they all agreed to branch with them, they dumped their former chiefs body in a nearby garbage can and set it on fire.

Gang chiefs who flipped their membership to the E.S.B. mob killed all members who protested. The gang chiefs who wouldn't bow down and flip, snuck out of town, out of fear of being murdered by one of their own members seeking a reward and to gain a crown over his mob from the E.S.B. The exiled gang chiefs vowed to come back to Chi-Town one day and seek revenge.

The whole purpose of the E.S.B. or die policy was to gain a monopoly over the city of Chicago's drug trade and eliminate all competition. The E.S.B. mob was originally just a few neighborhoods from out East, but blew up to them flipping the whole Eastside Black and Latino gangs. Gangs that was once opposition to each other, was now one Eastside mob united to take over the Southside and beyond.

After the wild 100's, the suburbs, and the whole Southside became branches of the mob the North and West side plugged in, calling themselves The E.S.B. North and West Factions. Ninety percent of the drugs on Chicago's streets were from them, with ninety percent of Chicago now being part of the E.S.B.

The E.S.B. or die policy paid off. They now had Chi-Town, N.I.U, and out-of-Towners from Minnesota, Indiana, Iowa, and beyond getting their drugs from them. They sought to take over the whole Midwest drug trade.

Narrator, Lucifer

All hail and praise to the ruler of all evil, the lord of money, the Hustle god. Yeah, it's your boy, the spirit of Err. Them E.S.B. boys got a plate full for real. Their captain was so happy he pulled it off, he went on and paid their connect off in the door. Now, the way them boys using them girls as test dummies, putting their lives in danger made me so proud, it almost brought tears to my eyes. I got to crown them with honorary horns. Especially Teno, he seen his cousin in need and put that bitch to work. Making her hide shit all in her crib and hustle to feed his nephew, that's my kind of family. When the Feds come bitch, we ain't related. Just do your bid and don't bitch or snitch.

The art of war is in full effect with that E.S.B. or die policy. They made the whole city flip by giving them the option money or death.

They feed the starving dogs winning their loyalty. Giving life to those who never lived. Making the poor niggas rich. The things people will do for money.

Money do change lives. Whoever said money couldn't buy happiness, only said it because they didn't have enough to buy it. To my mans, and them the E.S.B., the world is yours, starting with Chi-Town, then the whole Midwest baby. It's your boy L.G. closing out with my man Scarface the Rapper, "Money and the power, I ain't falling short cause I got money and the power yup."

Chapter 8

It was now time for Kareem to officially start school at N.I.U. Since he was the scholar out of the group, they put him in charge of all their finances. His job was to focus on laundering, investing, and washing the money while he oversaw their N.I.U. operation. They wanted him to maintain a low profile school-boy image while they multi-tasked.

Before sending him off to live on campus, they had a big off-to-college party for him at the House of Blues club. All you seen was Bentlys, Benzs, B.M.Ws, Range Rovers, Cadillac Escalade Trucks, and customized turtle-top Vans parked all around the House of Blues club in Chicago. Inside, all you seen was the authentic Gucci, Louis Vuitton, Prada, Fendi, and Dior while platinum and diamond jewelry lit up the club.

Everybody who was somebody was at the House of Blues club that night. It was flooded with the baddest bitches in town and every hood-rich, big-hat hustler. This was a Boss Stuna's party where they was stunting hard popping bottles and throwing money to show off their wealth. After the opening act left the stage Jay Z, Kanye West, and Rihanna performed with Big Face, Fats, Kareem, Teno, and Herby, their newest E.S.B. boss, on stage with them as if they were their entourage.

When they sang the part, "We gone run this town tonight," the whole crowd went crazy screaming, "The E.S.B. run this town!" all while they threw money. After they were done with the song, Rihanna who was looking real gothic wearing a black fishnet outfit showing off her sexy legs and butt, grabbed the mic and said in her Belgian accent, "Now everyone hold ya bottles up and drink to Kareem the basketball star going off to college."

Once again the crowd went crazy screaming, "E.S.B!" popping bottles, splashing champagne, and fizzing suds everywhere.

When the E.S.B. Bosses went to hang out in the V.I.P. section, they were greeted by five thick-lip, big-hip, big-booty, five-star groupies. After the ladies stripped naked, they began to suck and fuck on the E.S.B. Bosses. The ladies made their asses clap and shake in the men's faces and laps.

Their security men stopped two Italian men who were trying to bogart their way into the V.I.P. section. Herby approached the men and said, "Don't you see we busy! What the fuck do ya'll want?"

One of the Italians told him, "We know you fucking guys killed Mann. We come to get what belongs to us."

After Herby said, "What...What the fuck is you talking about? Is you fucking crazy?" he signaled for security to grab and escort the men out the club. When he went back and told the squad what the men said, they all jumped up to catch them outside the club.

When they ran up to the two Italians in the parking lot, one turned around smiling and said, "We know that's some of our shit on the streets plus we know what you all did. To settle this score like business men, we just want you guys to pay us what you owe us, and for you guys to do business with us from now on. Then you guys can go to sleep and wake up in peace. How about that fellas?"

Fats and Big Face pulled out their 44 and 45 magnum guns while Teno, Kareem, and Herby beat the men bloody beside a Van. Once they stopped beating the two men, Herby pulled out a razor and slit one of their throats.

Big Face told the other man, "Now go tell your boss we pay you pasta-eating boys nothing. It's E.S.B. or die bitch!" Then, he spit in the man's face before they all went back into the club.

After they washed the blood off themselves in the washroom, they went back out to party like nothing ever happened. When Jeezy got on stage to perform "The world is yours and everything in it," the police came in shutting the club down as they shouted, "The parties over everyone due to an incident."

The police found one man dead in the parking lot with no leads of why or by whom from anyone they questioned.

The E.S.B., with no further thoughts of the Italians, went home to get some rest so they all could get up early the next day to take Kareem to college.

Still hung over from the party last night, the E.S.B. along with an entourage of twelve E.S.B. members got up early to drive five cars deep to the college campus. When they pulled up to the dorm area and seen hundreds of fresh freshmen college girls moving in getting settled, they jumped out their vehicles to swarm the girls like sharks attacking.

Meanwhile, back in a Chicago eastside apartment building Tom

Tom, Little 'O', and Mike were in the kitchen mixing up dope and rocking up cocaine, while Mike weighed up some drugs on a scale for Little 'O' to bag up he said, "That nigga J.B. mad we don't cop our work from him no more. I told him we don't fuck with him no more cause my man Little 'O' say you got bullshit and if my mans say we ain't fucking with you no more that's what it is. Plus, Teno got my mans Little 'O' too shook to fuck with anyone else."

Little '0' responded, "Nigga if he got me shook, he got your punk-ass shook too. That nigga ain't never got me shook. He just got better, cheaper, shit. Matter of fact, you ain't got to fuck with us no more. You can get your shit from J.B. and do your own thang!"

Mike said, "Damn nigga, you ain't got to get all emotional with me. I ain't the one fucking the shit out of your baby momma and got you getting your work from your own B.M. I ain't got no problem working for your B.M. who works for another nigga whose beating her pussy up, fucking her all in her mouth and ass, do you?"

Little 'O' face turned furious as Mike and Tom Tom laughed hysterically.

Next, Mike said, "I ain't gon lie, I was laying on that ground next to you that day scared to death. I thought them young niggas was gone kill us. But we got up off that ground getting way more paper then we was before, so I love it. Aye man, I was just playing with you. But real talk, if I was you, I a be trying to use my B.M. to trick that nigga so we can come up harder. You don't give a fuck about that bitch no way, so work that bitch fool."

Little 'O' said, "Aye nigga, stop fucking playing with me! I don't give a fuck about that bitch, I got a gang of hoes. I know what the fuck I'm doing. You just sit back and watch. She Teno's girlfriend, but she gon always be my bitch, remember that. You need to be worried about Nicole instead of being all in my shit."

Tom Tom jumped in saying, "He don't need to be worried about her neither."

Little 'O' then winked an eye at Tom Tom when Mike wasn't looking and said, "Yeah, you don't need to be worried about her cause me and Tom Tom already stretched her out."

Mike, with an unsure look on his face said, "You niggas lying. Ya'll ain't did shit!"

"I took Tom Tom over there with me one day to drop some shit off to Tammy and my daughter, but they was gone over her mother's house. Nicole was the only one there and you know that bitch a stripper, so we smoked one with the hoe and paid her to strip for us. She got naked and gave us some of that super head like her name was Katt Stacks. Tom Tom hit the hoe in the ass while she gave me some head. We popped pills and ran train on the hoe all night. We had that pretty little red bone bitch working." Little 'O' said.

Tom Tom jumped in stating, "Her pink-ass pussy got so wet, it didn't make no sense."

Angrily, Mike interrupted them, "When this shit happen? Why you niggas ain't call me? That's some hating ass shit. Ya'll know I been wanting to push that bitch back in."

Tom Tom told him, "Nigga, what I'ma call you for when we got a bet on who gone fuck her first. I was gon tell you later after I grabbed her red hair and bobbed it one more time cause I know your trick-ass ain't gon want to share the hoe once you fuck her."

Mike was next to say, "Well, why Little 'O' fuck her?"

Tom Tom replied, "Cause he wasn't in our bet."

Now as Tom Tom and Little 'O' laughed hysterically, Mike stood there with a furious face. The three men finished bagging up their drugs and all went their separate ways to tend to their business.

Later that night, Little 'O' was riding around thinking about what Mike said earlier. Mike made him realize he was actually working for his baby momma who was working for another nigga who was fucking his bitch. He tried to reason with himself that, that wasn't the case, that they didn't make him look like a pussy, that he could still fuck her anytime he wanted, that he still controlled her, and that he could make her set Teno up if he wanted her to. After the E.S.B. made their house one of their major safe houses, Tammy no longer allowed Little 'O' to come over as he pleased and told him he had to call first, and then she would meet him on the porch. Little 'O' thought the reason he couldn't show up unannounced was because Teno was creeping with his baby momma. So, he decided to show up unannounced to see if he still had the power to get some pussy from her whenever he wanted. Regardless, if she gave him some or not, he planned to beat her up just to see if Teno would get involved.

When he got there and rang the doorbell, Nicole opened the door wearing just a robe.

He bogarted his way into the house yelling, "Tammy... Tammy...

Bitch, I know you hear me calling you!"

Nicole interrupted him saying, "Nigga, what's your fucking problem? Tammy's not here."

So, next he asked, "Well, where the fuck is my daughter?"

She answered, "First of all, watch who the fuck you talking to, and second ain't nobody here but me. I think Tammy at her mother's house and Teno and the rest of them all went to N.I.U. for a few days so I think you need to leave."

Little 'O' calmed down and said, "My bad, Nicole, I'm sorry. Just let me use your phone for a minute and I'm gone."

She said, "Alright. Just let yourself out when you done. I got to go finish watching my reality show."

When she left, Little 'O' grabbed the phone to call Tom Tom. When Tom Tom answered he said, "Aye nigga, how fast can you get to Tammy's house?"

Tom Tom told him, "One minute I'm around the corner."

"Good, cause I'm about to call Mike so we can piss him off." Little 'O' said. Then, he called Mike and once he answered he said, "Aye nigga, how fast can you get to Tammy's house?"

When he answered, 'in five minutes,' Little 'O' said, "Cause me and Tom Tom just got done running in Nicole. Nigga, if you want some, you better hurry up. You can't say we didn't call you this time." Then, he hung up just as Tom Tom came through the front door.

Soon as he was done telling Tom Tom the plan, Mike came through the door saying, "I thought you was on some bullshit until I seen on caller I.D. you calling from her house."

Little 'O' replied back, "Yeah nigga, we just got through running train on the hoe. We done, so we about to go, but you can have the bitch all to yourself now."

Tom Tom said, "Don't let her tell you no like you a lame or something, cause she a freak, she'll go."

Then, Little 'O' yelled, "Aye Nicole, I'm up, I'll holla at you later."

She yelled back, "Alright Little 'O' I'll see you later."

Mike locked the door behind them after they left.

When Nicole came into the living room and seen him, she said, "I thought Little 'O' just left, so why in the fuck is you in my house?"

He replied, "I just wanta see you take that robe off so I can see that pink ass of yours."

She responded back, "Mike, how many time do I got to tell you ain't shit gone ever happen with me and you. Now could you go run and catch your little friends?"

Mike got angry and said, "Why you be trying to play me like a lame? You gon give them some, but ain't gon give me none? You think I'm some type of goofy, huh?"

"I don't know what the fuck you talking about, but you got to go now," Nicole told him.

He grabbed her and threw her to the couch, and then said, "You gon give me some of this."

Nicole screamed, "Mike please stop... please stop... why you doing this to me?"

Mike snatched her robe off and raped her. When he was done raping her, he got up and said, "Why you tripping, you ain't shit but a little hoe anyway. Acting like you can't give a real nigga none of that."

Nicole laid there crying as he threw some money in her face and left.

Nicole called Erika and Tammy crying, telling them to come home right away. When Erika got home and found out what happened, and who did it, she ran to her room and came back out with an A.R.15 yelling, "Let's go murk them punk-ass niggas.

Just then, the front door opened and Tammy walked in. "What happened?" she asked.

Erika told her, "I told you to stop fucking with that punk-ass baby daddy of yours. He brought his punk-ass friend over here to rape our sister. So bitch, is you gon strap up or what?"

Tammy just stood there in shock for a minute and then grabbed her phone. "I'm calling the police. I should of been called them on Little 'O''s ass a long time ago."

Erika quickly snatched the phone out of Tammy's hand and said, "Bitch, we can't call the police. If they come search our house doing their investigation, we all going to jail." Then, she reached under the table by the couch and pulled out a pink pearl handle 25 automatic. She tossed the gun at Nicole and yelled, "Bitch, didn't I tell you in case of an emergency this was right here?"

Erika began to cry. "Why didn't you use it Nicole? Why didn't you shoot that bastard in his fucking head?" She dropped the A.R.15 to hug Nicole as she pulled out her cell phone to call Big Face.

Tammy, who was now on her phone talking to Little 'O', yelled, "I can't believe your bitch-ass did some shit like that. That's why you and your trifling ass friends going to jail. Don't ever say shit to me and you'll never see your daughter again."

Little 'O,' who was riding around in his truck with Tom Tom said, "Slow down, what the fuck is you talking about?"

She yelled back, "You bitch-ass nigga, don't try to act like you don't know what the fuck I'm talking about. You brought that nigga over here to rape her."

He then said, "Ooooh oh oh shiiit, he raped her? Tammy on everything I love, I ain't have shit to do with that. That nigga came over there when I was leaving. I ain't know what the fuck he wanted Nicole for so I left. Did she call the police?"

She answered, "Naw she ain't call the police, but you niggas still gon pay, so don't ever come over here again or say shit to me or your daughter again cause you gon get yours, nigga. I hate your ass!" She then hung up the phone.

Once Erika got off the phone with Big Face, she told them, "Big

Face said they on their way back right now. He said don't tell nobody shit, and number one don't call the police. He said he want all us to stay in the house to take care of Nicole until they get here, and he sending some of his goons over here to look after us until he get here."

When Little 'O' got off the phone with Tammy, he told Tom Tom everything she said. He then told him, "I didn't think he was gone rape the bitch. I thought he was just gon go in there and pull his dick out or something like that. Then make some sexual suggestions like bitch suck this or something and either come-up or make himself look like a damn fool. Then she'd kick him out and he'd know we sent him off. But not rape the bitch. He snapped out. She say they didn't call the police but I think they did."

Tom Tom said, "Yeah, I think they called the police. We need to fall back for a few days. This clown-ass nigga Mike got us hot. I'm about to call this goofy to see what was on his mind. He can't blame us for no shit like that."

Mike wouldn't answer the phone, so he left him a message saying, "Nigga you got us hot as hell. That bitch called the police. We ain't have shit to do with that, nigga. You can't blame us so don't involve us in that bullshit nigga." He then hung up and told Little 'O' in an angry tone, "This all your fault nigga. All because he struck a nerve when he told you the truth about your rat-ass baby momma."

Little 'O' looked at him with a confused face but remained silent.

The E.S.B. left Kareem at N.I.U. to rush back to the city. When they finally pulled up to the girls' house, they seen the goons they sent to secure the ladies posted up on their porch. Big Face instructed them to put a nationwide A.P.B. out for Little 'O' within the E.S.B. mob offering on Mike, Tom Tom, and Little 'O' a $50,000 reward for all three men.

The next day when Big Face, Fats, and Herby went to visit a B B.Q. event at Rainbow beach, two Chevy Impalas pulled up with Little Ray Ray and three other local E.S.B. members. When they got out of their cars, one anxiously yelled, "Fats, come check this shit out. We got a surprise for you, fam!"

When he walked over to one of the Impalas Little Ray Ray popped open the trunk and turned the sounds up so his speakers could kick out a Soulja Boy song "Speakers going hammer, burr burr burr..."

Fats' eyes got big as he looked inside the trunk and yelled, "aye Big Face... Herby... come check this shit out!"

When they came to look inside the trunk they seen Mike duck taped laying inside by a speaker box. Big Face then looked at Little Ray Ray and said, "You know the reward is for all three right?"

Little Ray Ray who was wearing a pair of bright red color skinny jeans that was sagging next did the Dougy dance as he opened the other Impalas' trunk with Little 'O' and Tom Tom ducked taped and tightly snugged in it.

Big Face smiled and told Fats, "Pay they little bad ass."

Little Ray Ray who was looking for more action looked at Fats and said, "I told Teno to let me do they ass when I had them face down/ass up in the street that day. I been wanting to do they ass. You got to let us torture these jerks for ya'll now."

One of the young guys with him name Baby 'D' said, "Yeah, let us take them to this place we call the torture chambers. We got some shit in there called the electric chair that a make you tell about shit you ain't even knew you knew about."

Herby looked the four young guys up and down and said, "What ya'll use to kill cats for fun when ya'll was babies? You little niggas got some serious issues. Ya'll fucked up in the head."

Big Face, who was now laughing said, "What the fuck is this world coming to? You got little niggas wearing skinny jeans doing the Dougy dance while they terrorize and torture the shit out of people... Ya'll close them trunks and follow us."

In a black Benz, they lead the Impalas to an alley as Fats called Teno who was at Erikas house and told him, "We need you to open the garage door, we pulling up in the ally now." The two chevys then pulled inside the garage while Big Face parallel parked the Benz in front of the garage as its doors closed.

Once they were all standing around the trunk, Little Ray Ray popped open the trunk. Teno picked the men up out the trunk, body slamming their bodies to the ground.

After that, Little Ray Ray once again told them how he caught them at a light in his Escalade so they trunked them.

Baby 'D' next told them, "After we trunked Little 'O' and Tom Tom, I jumped in the Escalade to follow our two Chevy's when all of a sudden this idiot Mike pulled up on me thinking I was them. So we jumped out to trunk his ass too."

Big Face instructed them to get their vehicles and bring them to the garage. Once they peeled out in the Chevy's, Teno brought Nicole into the garage for vengeance on their victims.

Once Nicole walked into the garage and seen Mike, she instantly attacked him with punches and kicks as she cryed and yelled, "You dirty nasty bastard I hate you!" Herby then handed her a bat that she used to knock Mike's teeth out and bust his head wide open. She next began to beat Little 'O' and Tom Tom with the bat until Herby grabbed the bat away from her and gave her a mallet hammer. She walked over to Mike and pulled his pants and boxer shorts down. She looked at his penis and laughed hysterically. "You got a good nut from this good pussy the other day, didn't you baby? But now off this you gone bust the best nut you ever had." She repeatedly slammed the mallet hammer down on his balls and penis until Tammy, who was holding an automatic 25 gun in her hand and Erika who was holding an AR15, banged on the garage door wanting in.

Teno grabbed Nicole to take her outside while Big Face snatched his AR15 away from Erika and went back inside the garage. Teno told Erika, "Cuz, calm the fuck down, we got this. Now take Nicole in the fucking house and don't come out no fucking more or I'm gone shoot you in your fucking weave... Now go!" He looked at Tammy and said, "Bitch, you too!

After the girls went into the house Little Ray Ray and Baby D' pulled up in the alley with Little 'O's truck and Mike's Cutlass. In the garage Big Face held the A.R.15 at Little 'O' and Tom Tom while Fats untied them and gave them both nine inch hunting knives. Teno then told them, "If ya'll don't kill that bitch we gone kill ya'll...Now handle that business. The men killed Mike by stabbing him 243 times. They then instructed them to put his dead body in the trunk of his own car and to leave it parked in front of his own house.

Mike's baby momma Janice noticed his Cutlass parked outside their apartment building but assumed he was riding around with Tom Tom or Little 'O'. When he failed to come home for two days she picked up the phone to file a missing persons report, but dropped the phone when she looked out the window to check on their seven year old son name Little Mike, who was with several of his friends pointing at some blood that was dripping from the trunk of his father's car. When the C.P.D. arrived, they found Mike's body stabbed to death in the trunk of his car. As they towed his car in for further investigation and test, Officer Johnson questioned Janice in her apartment asking her, "Who did he usually hang out with?" She held Little Mike in her arms and fought to hold her tears back as she answered, "The only people he hung out with everyday was no good ass Tom Tom and this sneaky bastard name Little 'O'." He next asked her, "Have you seen or heard from any of them since then?" She answered, "No... but I can give you their address, phone numbers, who their baby momma's are, and what kind of cars they drive... Officer, I use to tell him every day to stop hanging with them, they not your friends. But he wouldn't listen to me." She then broke down into tears.

'Narrator, Lucifer'

It's Lucifer signing in to give you some words of wisdom. A man's worst enemy is himself, so while you party goers busy partying you better watch what you do in life, watch how you speak, and watch how you move through the streets, cause that shit will come back to haunt you. If you don't believe me ask that bitch, Karma. If you ain't already know that shit they took from Mann to get where they at now, belonged to them Italians and they not trying to lose out on their investment. But let's see what happen cause the fat lady ain't sang yet. The spirit of Err once again signing out as A.K.A. Lucifer G, bitch!

Chapter 9

After the rape incident along with Mike's death, the E.S.B. along with the girls knew they had to tighten up on how they ran things. Also on how they responded to situations. No mistakes were allowed in this game, especially when they made it so far up because their fall would be much harder. This made them begin to make solid long term plans for themselves and their children.

The rape incident brought the girls more closer, made them untrusting of anyone outside their circle, more conscience of this worlds evils, and to focus on achieving their goals in life while they used the hustle game to help them finance it.

Erika started going to cosmetology school so she could open her own beauty salon one day. Nicole recovered well from the incident thanks to the closure she received in utilizing that mallet hammer. Hearing of Mike's brutal death afterwards is what really brought her peace of mind to move on in life.

She also began to take life more seriously by pursuing her dreams as a choreographer. She went back to school to gain a degree in dance. Most of the money she earned hustling for the E.S.B. she saved for her and her daughter. She also married her baby daddy, Iky, while he was still in prison serving a life sentence for a first degree murder, in hopes he would win his appeal and come back home to her. Tammy, on the other hand, was fed up with betrayal and abuse. She put up many emotional walls to protect herself, so she lived with distrusting the world.

She cut off all contact from Little 'O'. She'd seen life as a dog eat dog world so she became a dog. She started to fuck multiple hustlers, using them for what she could, playing the cut-throat game of Chicago's street life.

Teno continued to supply Little 'O' and Tom Tom who maintained their drug operation after Mike's death as if nothing ever happened. They stayed out of the E.S.B's way and did what they were told. Little 'O' couldn't take not seeing his daughter Cece anymore. He figured Tammy was Teno's girl so if anyone could convince her to allow him to see his daughter again it was him. Since Teno was on his way over to collect some money, he decided to ask him for his help. By Teno being a Father also he agreed to help him as much as he could. Because he hated baby momma's who kept their kids away from their fathers out of spite. He didn't wish that on no one, not even his worst enemy. Convincing her wasn't easy, but she eventually compromised to dropping Cece off over his house on weekends.

***

Kareem was a very important man. He was a basketball star plus an E.S.B. boss. They couldn't afford for anything to happen to him especially with him being in charge of all their finances. They put twelve E.S.B. members who also attended N.I.U, on his personal security. Twelve men following you around would usually make people suspect something, but by him being a basketball star, they knew everyone would think they were just his entourage hanging with him due to his fame.

Kareem couldn't let his name get caught up in any illegal activities if he wanted to make the N.B.A. draft. To stay low key he put an Iranian boy name Husain in charge of their off campus drug operation. Husain was from the North side of Chicago, who you would swear was a black dude due to his swag. Kareem first met him when they attended the Nike summer basketball camp. Husain wasn't much of a hooper but he was indeed a true hustler. He use to smuggle pounds of weed into the camp to sell every summer. One summer some guys attempted to beat him out by getting some weed on credit promising to pay later. When he went to collect, they didn't have his money. So he went to get a 22 long gun from Kareem, who took it from Big Face to sneak into camp. When Husain ran up on the boys shooting, some camp supervisors tackled him and took the gun. When they asked him where he got the gun from he told them he brought it from his home. He was then barred from ever attending camp again and sent home with no charges. Kareem found out Husain was now a sophomore here at N.I.U, and had it locked on the weed business, so he offered his long time friend a job. Once he accepted the job he laid a strict chain of command rule down. Kareem was now able to focus on school and basketball with Husain in charge.

Kareem, once Simeon High schools star shooting guard is now N.I.U's starting shooting guard who is well worth the full scholarship he received. He led them to many N.C.A.A. victories. The most memorable win was by 42 points against U.C.L.A. where he scored 33 points, 11 rebounds, and 12 assists amassing a triple double. Alabama state, Kentucky state, and Tennessee state all continuously offered him full scholarships to transfer to their school. He refused to part from his brotherhood, so he never told them about the offers because he knew they would make him go.

Kareem did well and got good grades in all his classes. But, he became frustrated because he didn't have any free time. Off the record, one of his coaches set him up with a tutor name Kimberly, that all the teacher would turn a blind eye to when she sat in to take his exams. She was a white girl who was a junior at N.I.U. She was infatuated with Kareem. All she wanted to do was give him brain in return for her using her brain in his classes. She was a groupie who wanted to be able to say she had a basketball star in her mouth. If he made it to the N.B.A. she could then proudly watch his games and say she know how he taste. He never fucked her but after every exam she would come over to his dorm room to suck on the head of his dick with her tongue ring on until he nutted in her face.

He had a thick black girlfriend on campus name Alexus who also had a thick black girlfriend name Ass-in-martina. Every day he enjoyed ménage à trois with his girlfriend and her girlfriend. They were fully aware that they had to share him with his tutor Kimberly. But, they didn't mind as long as she got him all A's and B's in all his classes. Thanks to his tutor, he now had free time to indulge in other things.

Kareem then masterminded many ways to clean up their money in multiple business ventures. He wanted his brothers to retire from the game once he made it to the N.B.A. He knew if he couldn't make them rich legitimately investing this money now, it would never happen. Kareem next hooked up with an Asian boy on campus they called Ching-Chung-Chew who was a natural born genius. Ching-Chung-Chew had an ingenious idea with no resources to get it up and running. Kareem offered to provide all the finances if he gave him a 52%

partnership. Kareem and Ching-Chung-Chew then created a very profitable internet-gambling site that changed all their lives. If he gave up on school and basketball now he would still be set for life. He began to invest putting record companies, Hotels, Car lots, Buildings, and etc, in the E.S.B. name for them to prosper.

All their money may have been tied up in these investments for the moment but it was guaranteed to pay off in the end, allowing them an opportunity to retire from the game forever.

One of the business ventures Kareem invested in was a record label called, East Side or Die Records. All of them were shared owners in the company but Herby was the chief C.E.O who ran it. Herby was instructed not to touch or deal any drugs at the company during workday office hours. He was only to hustle out of it on weekends when he was renting studio time out to artist so no employees would be around. But instead of conducting serious recording sessions, Herby conducted parties there every day. The few Chicago artists the label did have signed, didn't realize the delay in finishing their demo's due to all the partying they were doing, where the drug of your choice was plentiful. Herby became your modern day Suge Knight of the recording industry. He was assaulting his artists, making them sign bogus contacts, never paying them their advances or royalties, nor was he completing the recording of their demo's. All he did was hold parties in the studio where everyone walked around with powder on their noses, strippers everywhere, and mountains of cocaine piled up on plates for the guess to Scareface. All his parties had cocaine, herion, ecstasy pills, lean, cush weed, Hennessy, 211, Grey Goose, V.S.O.P, and you name it he had it there. When he was supposed to be conducting business, you could find him nodded out off dope in a recording both. Herby had a dope habit with heroin he established in his early stick up years that he had been recently clean. But now, with the unlimited access to it all, he relapsed. His cravings resurfaced with a growing appetite. He was so far gone that he could be in the middle of a conversation with you and would nod out while he still stood on his feet. The man would literally be asleep standing up and would actually wake up finishing the sentence he nodded out to. Partying with drugs and whores was how he spent the majority of his days. He was fucking up large amounts of drugs with his expensive partying. To make up for the loses with the drugs, he began to blow it up and hit it; cutting it with mixes he had no business mixing it with. It got to the point where he would sell a dealer a large amount of drugs then put a mask on to rob him for them back. One thing was for sure was, he always had his share of the cop money to turn in, so none of his fellow E.S.B. bosses would know he was fucking up. The one time he didn't have his share of the cop money, he ran in a drug house out west by himself and killed everyone inside. When he came out, he had his share of the money plus eighty grams of heroin. One day he sold an E.S.B. member name Sambo and his crew 1000 grams of heroin and two keys of cocaine that was no good. The dope had already fallen off, it couldn't be hit, and the two keys of coke only had nine ounces of real cocaine in it. Sambo and his crew reported the incident to Big Face demanding action be taken against Herby.

All he did was reimbursed them with a good 1000 grams of heroin and two keys of coke plus two pounds of cush weed for their troubles. When he reimbursed them with no objections to their allegations against a boss, they knew he wasn't going to do anything about it. Sambo and his guys felt like Herby disrespected their gangsta by playing them like punks. So now, they plotted to teach Herby that they were indeed true motherfucking gangsters that you dare not cross.

Big Face didn't want to believe it but he suspected Herby was back messing around with that dope. Some employees along with an artist from their label began reporting Herby's lude, unprofessional actions and activities to the other C.E.O's of E.S.B. Records. Big Face convinced himself that he had it under control, that his actions wasn't detrimental to them, their business, or himself, until he along with the other bosses started to find out about the robberies and murders he was suspected to have committed. Kareem was even hearing about them all the way at N.I.U. and knew they had Herby's handwriting all over them. One minute you'll be buying some weight from him then the next you're being robbed. Everyone knew, but no one could for a certainty blame Herby for them. But now, with Sambo and his crew reporting how he beat them out to everyone, the streets now had the proof to link and blame him for a lot more.

Now that the cat was out the bag and presented to the bosses they knew action had to be taken. He was jeopardizing everything they had built. It was either Herby fall or they all fall. So now, as much as it hurt them to do what needed to be done, they all finally agreed to give him a death violation. They all loved him dearly but knew he was out of control. They put a time limit on the violation agreeing that with their aid and assistance that if he didn't get his act together 100% within thirty days, the death violation would be carried out immediately. They all wanted to believe he would get it together, but deep down, they knew he had only thirty more days to live.

Some of the E.S.B. investments Big Face was in charge of was a Chrysler dealership and a couple of hotels near Midway airport. Big Face now portrayed himself as a legit businessman while he ran his underworld mob that had a major pipeline of narcotics being fed to them by the Nigerians and Mexican mafia. To fully play the businessman's   role he began dressing in casual wear, suits, and driving luxury cars and trucks. When he wasn't doing business, he was with his girlfriend and daughter enjoying family time while he spoiled them with the finer things in life.

Big Face and his girlfriend Keshia had a loving relationship but it wasn't perfect thanks to an estrange woman name Renae who got pregnant by him. Renae, who lived on 78th and Cottage Grove, is a yellow-bone female, five feet tall, 140 pounds, with a 36-24-47 figure, short black hair, juicy lips, and the prettiest face you ever seen. Whenever Big Face was running the streets and had free time, he would pull up to her house blowing the horn hoping she'd invite him in. Once inside it would never fail, after they smoked a couple blunts and drank some Hennessy she would pull his dick out, rub it all over her pretty face until he got rock hard, slapping her in the face with it. Every time he slapped her face with his dick she would say, "Hit me harder baby." After that she would grab his dick and massage his balls while kissing and licking all over his dick, rubbing her juicy lips all over it. After she kissed, licked, and just sucked on the head of his dick for a while, he would grab her short hair to fuck her in the mouth. When looking down at her pretty face and juicy lips going up and down on his dick he couldn't help but to come in her mouth, then pull it out to grind on her face to finish nutting on her lips and face. She had him so sprung off the head that he couldn't help but spoil her with cars, clothes, jewelry, money, and whatever else she wanted he got it for her. He was so caught up in her head game he couldn't ever recall hitting the pussy, so he had no idea how she got pregnant by him when he stayed nutting in her mouth. When she told him she was pregnant by him, he told her, "Bitch stop lying! I ain't never fuck you. That damn baby ain't mine. Stay the fuck away from me, you cut off."

Nine months later, she popped up at his condominium downtown knocking on his door with a baby boy. When Keshia opened the door, Renae said, "I didn't come here to start no trouble. I know you Big Face's baby momma but this his son and all I want for him to do is take a blood test and take care of his son.

Out of respect, me and him don't have to have no contact, we can go through you. I just want him to do his part."

When Keshia looked at the baby who looked just like Big Face, her heart dropped. She didn't know what to say so she just invited them in to wait for him to come home.

Once Big Face finally came walking through the front door, he seen his daughter Alivia playing with a little baby on the floor. Then he noticed Keshia staring at him with a face of disgust saying real slow, "Now before you say anything to me... we gone all get into your car... to get a blood test."

Once he seen Renae in the living room, he knew to remain quiet, so he lit up a blunt and did as he was told. Remaining quiet made the situation more awkward and uncomfortable, but he was still at ease because he just knew that baby wasn't his until the Doctor came out announcing he is the father.

Once Keshia pulled herself back together from hearing the news she laid the rules down to Renae, "Now that we know this his son, I will make sure he do his part, but everything will go through me. I don't want him to have no contact with you. So, through me, I'll make sure you get a check every week to take care of him. Also on his birthdays and holidays, if it's alright with you, I'll pick him up to spend time with his father and to get to know his sister."

Renae, feeling relieved, said, "I don't have a problem with that. That's all I was asking for anyway."

Now, to deal with the hurt and pain, Keshia didn't say a word to him for over two weeks and just buried herself in her daily activities.

Big Face assured her that it was just a one-night stand that would never happen again, so she eventually forgave him and accepted his son, believing his love was true to only her.

He became a loving family man at home, but once in them streets, he transformed into a beast becoming America's worst nightmare. Big Face was living the American dream. He was doing well in his legal and illegal business. The Nigerians and the Mexican mafia loved him. With all the money he brought them, how could they not love him? Life was good, but the moment was soon arriving where he knew he had to chose of either claiming his crown as king of taking over the Midwest drug game or going legit retiring from the game and never looking back.

When that time does come for him to make that decision it would be one that affects many.

Fats was put in charge to oversee E.S.B. realtors, which stood for Estates, Studios, and Buildings. They renovated and sold property all over the state of Illinois. Fats enjoyed his rich high life as a boss. After all the blood, sweat, prison bids, and murders he finally made it. Things were going well and he enjoyed the best of both worlds, the legal and illegal side. Fats went from rags to riches, from hoodrats to top of the line freaky flawless model bitches.

One day, Fats was doing an inspection on one of the 16-unit apartment buildings E.S.B. realtors owned on the far eastside of Chicago, when he noticed one of the tenants was a woman name Gelisa who he use to have a childhood crush on. He used to chase her around trying to freak on her when they were youngsters, until her older brother Diablo beat him up and chased him off.

Gelisa was a pretty Puerto Rican woman who looked like a five foot five inch tall, Jennifer Lopez with long hair to her butt, but she was never a Jenny off the block. When she came out of her apartment and he called her name, he was surprised she remembered who he was. After ten minutes of talking and flirting with each other they exchanged phone numbers.

Before she left he asked her, "Where you rushing out to?"

She said, "I got to go visit my brother Diablo at Stateville."

He told her, "Tell him I said what's up." She responded, "I sure will." and left the building.

Diablo, who was affiliated with the King gang, was currently incarcerated at Stateville Correctional Center serving two natural life sentences for killing five men at Bowen High school six years ago. He was a dedicated gangbanger. I don't care what gang you was in or how many people was with you when he came around, everyone left out of fear. He had over thirty murders under his belt. He killed in broad daylight in front of crowds. But, nobody would ever say a word out of fear, until he cold bloodedly shot dead them five boys in front of Bowen High school. Diablo was a six foot three inch tall, 310 pound, cock strong Puerto Rican with a bald head, who was tattooed from head to toe. His face was even tattooed. He had devil horns tattooed on his head with a king's crown going all around his head. Diablo earned his name for he was truly the devil in the flesh. He was serving his time at a maximum-security prison called Menard until he caught a jail house case, three attempt murder charges for stabbing two inmates and a Correctional Officer for trying to stop him.

Diablo sister on the other hand was the complete opposite from him. He was the Devil and she was an angel. She was a good girl who graduated from Washington High school on the honor roll. Diablo provided for her, protected her, and beat down anyone who looked at her wrong. He served as her guardian angel if that's what you want to call it. She had to sneak around with her boyfriends if she didn't want her brother to beat them up and run them off. She never knew it but her brother killed one of her boyfriends when they were young for coming over their house to visit her. He beat the boy to death and left his body in an alley three blocks away. If you ever knew a true killer, he was him.

When Gelisa went to visit Diablo at Stateville she told him how she ran into Fats. How he was the new owner of her building and that he asked her to tell him, "What's up." The muscles in his head made the two devil horns twitch as he sat silently in the visiting room for a moment in deep thought from what she just told him. He remembered Fats from the hood and been hearing about his E.S.B. crew in which he respected their style to the upmost. He was always protective of his sister, but now he insinuated and influenced her indirectly to get with Fats. He plotted to pimp his sister to Fats without her realizing it.

Gelisa and Fats went out on several dates maintaining a friendly, but flirtatious, relationship. This was all until she refuse to allow him to drive home from her apartment one night when he became drunk. She then led him into her bedroom, laying him in her bed, taking his shoes off, then leaving him to rest. When she went back into the room to check on him, he grabbed her hand, pulling her to the bed where she willingly laid on top of him and began kissing him passionately, while she took his shirt off. Once she stripped him and herself naked, she began to ride him nice and slow until the freak came out making her ride him vigorously, moving faster and harder, while she leaned her head back moaning. As she bounced up and down on his dick, he thought to himself, she got the bomb, her pussy good and tight. She then squeezed her pussy muscles making it tighter, as she clawed his chest and had an orgasm, letting her pussy juices come down on him hard.

Fats then turned her over and said, "Now it's my turn"" He wrapped her long hair around one of his hands, making a fist, while she tooted her ass up in the air, grabbing one of her butt checks to spread for her pussy to open up for him to enter. He shoved his dick deep inside her and pulled on her hair, fucking as if he was riding a wild horse. She began to moan and say freaky things to him in Spanish. It may have sounded real sexy to him but he didn't have a clue as to what she was saying. He would be ramming her pussy in from the back one minute, then the next fucking her nice and slow giving her every inch of him while he felt all of her enjoying her tight, warm, wetness. They fucked all night until they fell asleep locked inside each other as one. Two weeks later when she told him she was pregnant, he bought a condominium next to Big Face to live with her. He became a true sucker for love,

Fats went with Gelisa to visit her brother Diablo many times and gained a close relationship with him. Once Diablo explained the technicalities in his case and what it would take to get him out, Fats agreed to put the money up to pay for his legal expenses. Seven months after that date Diablo received from the Supreme Court of Illinois an order for his immediate release from prison. Diablo was instantly recruited by the E.S.B. bosses. He was now in debt to them for helping him. He was also a natural born killer who they needed on the squad. Diablo was in no way a hustler, he couldn't get no money if you put it in his face. They utilized him by making him their Chief of Security (C.O.S.) for the E.S.B. mob. He now had the job of his dreams, a killer on the payroll.

Teno was in charge of a club downtown and a giant mall out east on 95th and Stony Island Ave, where they rented space to different vendors and stores. It was called, The Eastside's Big Bargain Mall, The E.S.B.M.

Teno also enjoyed his life as a boss playing the business game and the exciting never sleeping drug game that he was now a major player in. He was always a player who all the bitches loved, but now with the money and power bitches fought to suck his dick, trying to get his nut in any hole they could.

The bitches in Chicago knew he had an uncontrollable appetite for random women, so they used that, plotting to get into his pockets with a baby. He couldn't go nowhere without some bitches claiming they were pregnant by him or that this was his baby.

He was a walking Maury show because every time the results came back, it said, "Teno is not the father." He loved and spoiled the two daughters he named Nikki and Tiffany; they were his little princesses. He didn't mess around with his baby mommas much but he would throw them some crumbs hoping it would keep them out his face.

They did what every Chicago bitch who wished they had a baby by him wished they could do. They used their child to get into his pockets.

One of Teno's baby mommas called him over one day claiming his child was crying for him to come over, but when he got there, she was all alone with lingerie on playing with her pussy. Teno not being strong enough to fight his cravings for pussy, fucked her every time she tricked him over. It was like his baby mommas traded notes because the other one would get him the exact same way. The only difference was this one would aggressively pull his dick out to put in her mouth before he made it in the house good. She literally tried to suck him back into her life. They always used their child name, claiming they needed money for this and that, it was always something. They would tell him, "I need you to pay my rent this month, unless you wanta see me and your daughter kicked out on the streets." These bitches was on welfare with child care and day care paid for by the state, but instead they would tell him, "I need some money for her day care and doctor bill."

They sucked, fucked, and schemed him out all they could. He told himself he would never get them bitches pregnant again. Having another baby by them gold digging, money-sucking hoes was a big No, No! He regretted getting them pregnant and that they were the mother of his daughters, but he didn't regret his daughters. He loved them and was glad he had them, but wished it was just by better women.

Teno was prey to every bitch. It got so outrageous that bitches were running around town selling sex tapes with them starring Teno. They even had pictures and shots on their phones of themselves performing sex acts on him going around town.

He was hot like those R. Kelly and Ray J. with Kim Kardasian sex tapes. Bitches would give him some head and hold the nut in their mouth, saving it to put inside their pussy later. If he nutted in a bitch ass, she would drain her ass to put it in her pussy. They would put his nut in turkey basters trying every trick they could think of to get his baby, but the only baby Teno was going to put in a bitch stomach was from her mouth.

On a Saturday night the E.S.B. bosses would wine down to enjoy their downtown club investment that Teno oversees. Once you made it pass the security checkpoint, and pass the oversize bouncers, the doors would open up to an enormous dim club that was lit up by flashy multicolor smoke screens. Now as the E.S.B. bosses entered the club, as if gliding on clouds in their expensive Maury shoes, clubbers would greet and praise them as if they were gods. On their stroll the bosses would strut past a giant fish tank with four naked mermaids who continuously fondled each other. Once they made it to the center floor of the club they would check out the nude women in body paint swinging above them, then small talk with some clubbers and flirt with a few ladies. They next journeyed to the bar grabbing bottles of Gold Moet and Chandon from some topless female bartenders who was also covered in body paint. After that, they stopped at the stripper pole section to throw money at some thick beautiful strippers who slid down the pole. The strippers were doing all types of tricks with their pussies, making their ass's clap, and giving exclusive lap dances. When they went into the co-ed bathroom to freshen up they were greeted by topless female servants who would if you paid them for it, shake your dick after you pissed and even wipe your ass after a shit. They also did shaves, sold ties, condoms, and other necessities, while they squirted soap on your hands, rinsed, then dried them for you.

Once they were done in the restroom, instead of heading up to the luxurious V.I.P. section where you would be catered to by topless servants, they stepped down to the basement where it was invites only to enter its private casino. In the casino, area Chi-Town top hustlers placed bets of hundreds of thousands on craps, blackjack, and poker. You name it they betted on it. The female card dealers in the casino were even topless. The world was now a big casino with the E.S.B. rolling the dice, riding their luck, trying to break the bank.

'Narrator, Lucifer'

How could America's nightmare be living the American dream? I guess that's just the American way. Yeah, E.S.B. should stand for 'Venni Veta Vicci!' That's Itailan for, I came, I saw, I conquered. They conquered the eastside, the whole city, and most of the Midwest, but what about the eastside of Hades, cuz that's my block... It's that dude Lucifer G. the spirit of Err and I'm up bitches!

Chapter 10

On a Saturday night, at the E.S.B. downtown club, Big Face, Fats, Teno, and Herby sat up front by the stripper stage getting lap dances while four other strippers on stage performed to a Rihanna song, "Oh na na, what's my name..."

One of the strippers then hung upside down from a pole, spreading her legs wide open, as another stripper ate her pussy. As the crowd made it rain on stage with money from the explicit sight, two men with dreadlocks jumped onto the stage, pushed the strippers out the way, aimed and shot their automatic hand guns at the E.S.B. bosses, who was sitting up front with strippers still dancing on their laps. When Herby saw the shooters shooting, he put the stripper who was sitting on his lap in the full-Nelson lock, using her body as a human shield. She took two shots to her upper chest as they fell to the ground still in the chair. All the E.S.B. bosses fell to the floor, escaping the spray of bullets that was intended to exterminate their existence. When the two assassins ran up to the end of the stage for some close range shots at them who was now on the ground curled up with the strippers like it was cuddle time, security ran up shooting one of them in his back shoulder area, causing him to turn around and hesitate while his accomplice turned around shooting. Once the other assassin shook the shot off he took, like it was nothing, they charged security with shots, shooting their way out the club. As they ran out the clubs door backwards still shooting their guns, Big Face snatched a 12 gauge shot gun from one of the security men to shot one of the assassins, knocking him through the doors, leaving his body outside the club with a hole in his chest. The other assassin escaped to the parking lot, burning out in a super Charge Charger, while Chicago's police flashed its lights behind him, beginning a high-speed chase. In this fast and furious chase the assassin tried to make a sharp right turn with 148 M.P.H. on the dash and flipped the whip several times leaving pieces of his body and dreadlocks scattered all over the road.

Back inside the club, people where running around frantically stampeding over each other in attempts to get out the best way they could. Big Face gave the shotgun back to security and fled with his fellow bosses. They knew many men where enemies of theirs, but for sure only one of their foes had the money and connect to hire them professional Jamaican hitters to come for their lives.

After the club incident on a Monday afternoon, Big Face was working in the back receiving area of his Chrysler dealership. He was taking inventory on some cars coming in off the trucks, when one of his employees came running in telling him that they were having some problems with three men up front. Meanwhile, upfront in the showroom, three Italian men banged on a show room car, while one said, "Tell your boss we want to test drive the car with the money he owe us in it." An employee then told him, "I just called the police, so when they get here you can tell them what car you want them to test drive you all to jail in." One of the angry Italian men then picked the employee up and tossed him through the big showroom window. When Big Face made it up front, the men were already gone.

Later that day during rush hour, Herby was driving home on the Dan Ryan Expressway, from finally doing a real day of work at East Side or Die Records, when a blue G.M.C. truck pulled up beside him shooting Mac 11 shells. Herby who already had a plate full of cocaine with a nine Beretta gun on his lap, instantly got to shooting back before he swerved out the traffic jam unto the Dan Ryan's shoulder to escape the hail of bullets. In his rearview mirror, he seen the blue G.M.C. behind him, then his back window shattered from the shots of a man hanging out the truck's window. As they pursued him in a chase on the shoulder, Herby bust shots back every time they paused from their shots. With the Dan Ryan being congested with a traffic jam, Herby desperately looked for an opening in traffic and prayed the shoulder remained clear as they hit high speeds of 160 M.P.H. and rising. All of a sudden, Herby heard sirens and seen the flashing lights of a State Trooper car behind the truck, now in the chase on the Dan Ryan's shoulder the only path clear. Herby suddenly spotted a tight squeeze through traffic and took it. He banged his car up pretty badly but managed to get up out of there to escape on a nearby ramp.

The blue truck was too big to swerve through the traffic, so they continued on the shoulder until the Troopers car crashed, which allowed them to ram their way through traffic to escape.

During the week on a Wednesday at 3:15 P.M, Teno stood in front of Bradwell Elementary school waiting on his daughter Nikki to come out while he flirted with a very nice looking woman who was also at the school to pick up her daughter.

When Teno's daughter came out of the school walking towards him, a brown Regal rode up the block with heavy assault weapons hanging out the window shooting in Teno's direction. He ran to grab Nikki, shielding her body with his own, as he dove beside his car.

While his car rocked back and forth from the hail of ongoing bullets it received, he upped and tightly gripped the handle of his 38 short gun as he laid on top of Nikki hoping it will stop any bullets trying to harm his seed.

When the Regal finally rode up the block and turned the corner, Teno got up off Nikki to see if she still had life. Once he seen they both escaped the wrath of choppers chopping, he noticed his car was completely totaled with bullet holes piercings all through it. He noticed the woman he was just talking to laying on the ground suffering from a shot to the leg.

Tears began to fall from Teno's eyes when he witnessed a crowd in front of the school building screaming and yelling as a male teacher held a bleeding shot up little girl in his arms. Teno looked down the street and yelled, "I'ma show you bitches what war is! On my kids, you bitches gone pay one hundred times greater for this. I promise you that... I fucking promise you that!"

Fats got a call from his baby momma Gelisa who was crying, begging him to come home saying, "Some guys been calling here all day asking for you saying either you pay them what you owe with money or your life." He told her, "Don't answer the phone no more and don't leave. I just got to make one more run and I'll be there." She said, "Alright baby, just be careful. I love you." He replied, "Yeah, alright." and hung up. He then went to the B's to check on his man Crunch who ran the spot for him on 85th and Burnham. When he pulled up on the block he seen all the workers just sitting on the porch so he asked,

"What the fuck is ya'll doing?"

One of them responded, "Crunch ain't here to give us our work or open the door."

As Fats opened the door he said, "I wonder why this nigga left his car in the driveway?"

Once the door swung all the way open they all just stood there in shock for a moment staring at Crunch's dead body hanging from the ceiling, with, 'Pay Me' spray painted on his shirtless body that was battered.

One of the workers next said, "It's a note stuffed in his mouth."

So, Fats pulled it out reading its contents that read, "if you want this to stop, reimburse me for the two things you took, Mann and my shit."

After the Italians made several attempts on their lives, the E.S.B. bosses along with Diablo their C.O.S, all met at a safe house to figure out a war strategy that would heinously destroy their Italian problem forever. But, there was a major obstacle stopping them from marching forward; the enemy was like the Taliban. They knew it was the Italian who supplied Mann, but they didn't have a face behind it. They only knew why their enemies struck and what their enemies were. They had no idea where their enemies was, or who all their enemies were. This left them like U.S. troops being attacked by ghost, waiting on the Taliban to show its face so they could fight back.

They finally got a breakthrough when they found Chuck who was more than willing to help. Chuck use to work for Mann until she pistol whipped him, and shot his homie at a dice game for allegedly fucking up her money. Since Chuck used to be Mann's right hand man, running her drug spots, always being with her and tending to her business, he had all the missing pieces to the puzzle. He unveiled who they all were and where they all be, helping the E.S.B. now know how and when to attack. Diablo then gathered some soldiers and went to stalk their prey, so he could strategize a plan full of missions that would leave death with all their enemies.

Back at a Chicago's police station forensic lab, the finger prints that was found on Mike's car came back a positive match identifying Little 'O' and Tom Tom with their pictures showing up on the screen. The police department was told to bring the two men for questioning.

Little 'O' and Tom Tom was picked up during a routine traffic stop and was now in two different interrogation rooms being interrogated by Homicide Detective Mr. Walls and Mr. Burns for the murder of twenty six year old Mike Myer. As Little 'O' told the two Detectives his alibi for the seventh time, Detective Walls told him, "You know you done fucked up right?" Then, he pointed his finger in Little 'O's face and continued "Because you just told us somethin, different... You ain't even catch what you told us different, but we did... yeah you done fucked up now... You know it's over right? You fucked up."

Little 'O' got to stuttering, "Wwwwhat I sssay dif dif dif different. I didn't sssay nununu nothing different dididi did I? Cuz see what I meant to say was..."

Detective Walls then interrupted him by banging on the table saying, "Shut the fuck up!

You already fucked up. It's too late. You about to be somebodies bitch in the joint. So get ready to buy a lot of grease from commissary unless you ready to cooperate with us. Now when we come back in, in fifteen minutes you tell us if you gone cooperate or buy grease." as they left the room Det. Burns looked back and said, "You know you done fucked up don't you!"

The Homicide Detectives next entered the interrogation room with Tom Tom. Detective Burns told him, "Your B.F.F. or shall I say your best fucking friend Little 'O' just saved his own ass by telling on you. You know he gone get on the stand and tell it all SO he won't go to prison for the rest of his life like you. But you'll be alright cause you gone be Big Bubba's bitch making sweet sweaty love with him. That's what you want right? Because if not, you need to tell us something better than he did... I tell you what, let's play who can tell the best to get the get out of jail prize." Tom Tom then said, "What that nigga tell ya'll?" Detective Burns said, "Naw, Tommy-Tom, the rules to the game isn't what he told us but what you can tell us that you think is better, so you can win the get out of jail card, cause right now your best fucking friend is winning."

Tom Tom shook his head and just stared at the floor silently. Detective Burns then stated, "We gone give you fifteen minutes to think about how Little 'O' is such a good friend for sending you up the river to have sweet sweaty sex with Big Bubba and to see if you got that get out of jail winning answer." As the two Detectives walked out the room Detective Walls looked back at him, blew a kiss and said, "Smoochies" before slamming the door shut.

When the Detectives went back into the room with Little 'O', Detective Walls asked him, "Grease or cooperation?"

He responded, "Niether, I'll take your wife's mouth instead."

Detective Walls then began to continuously slam Little 'O's head on the table. When he stopped, Little 'O' said, "You bitches gotta kill me." Detective Walls replied, "O.K. we will."

Detective Burns next held him from behind while Detective Walls kicked him in the nuts.

Little 'O' then screamed in a high pitch voice, "O.k, o.k, o.k, o.k, o.k, I'll tell you."

When Detective Walls stopped kicking him he said, "I promise I'll tell you everything. Just let me talk to Tom Tom for five minutes first." They just looked at him while he held his nuts before they walked out the room.

As soon as Detective Burns walked into the room with Tom Tom he punched him in the face and began choking him. He then asked him, "Do you got something to tell us before it's over?" He responded, "Just let me holla at Little '0'." Detective Burns grabbed him by his legs and drug him out the room to Little 'O's room to sit them beside each other. The Detectives then sat on the other side of the room and watched them whisper to each other.

Tom Tom looked at Little 'O' and said, "Your bitch ass told them I did it. Nigga, what the fuck did you tell them?"

He replied, I ain't tell em' shit. All I said was let me holla at you first."

Tom Tom replied, "What... what the fuck you mean holla at me first? Your pussy ass ain't about to put this shit on me."

Little 'O' explained, "Naw, Nigga Teno... all we did was get rid of the body for him so he wouldn't kill us next... You with me?"

He answered, "Yeah... Fuck Teno."

Detective Walls then asked, "Are you two bitches ready to talk or what?"

They both answered, "Yeah, we ready to talk."

Once they told the Homicide Detectives that Teno killed Mike and made them get rid of the body they ran Teno's name through the system and had them identify him through pictures. Once the Detectives found out Teno was under Federal investigation, they called Federal Agent Shabazz. After Agent Shabazz questioned the two men, he informed the Detectives that the Feds were taking over this murder case and that the two men were now working as C.I's, confidential informants.

***

Sambo, with four of his guys, rode four cars deep flashing around town, showing off their new Corvette, Camero S.S, Dodge Challenger, and Mustang 5.0. G.T. that was customized with candy paint, 28 inch rims, T.V's, sound systems, the whole works. After bending most of Chi-Town blocks stunting their whips, they decided to stop at Grant Park to holla at some females. They flossed their new jewelry and gear that was fresh to death from the top of their fitted caps all the way down to the red bottom sole of their shoes. Before exiting their cars, they hit the stash boxes in the whips to get the guns out. Sambo always told his squad, "We gotta always keep our swords on us, so we be prepared when jealousy influences a broke nigga to try us." They strapped up and hoped out the Whips spitting game at the honeys like pimps from the 70s.

While Sambo peeped, he was being chosen by a group of black and Latino females he noticed a crowd of Italians having a picnic. He immediately called Diablo stating, "You need to get here at Grant Park. I just spotted a group of unfamiliars who could be them ghost. So you need to identify, because we still don't know who the Mad Rapper is, but you do and we don't want to blindly let em go, you feel me?" He responded with, "Amor" and hung up.

Once Diablo showed up at Grant Park identifying the Italians as the ones Chuck pointed out to him, when they went to spy on them, he called Herby. Sambo hated Herby and had been waiting on the opportunity to retaliate against him for selling them some bogus drugs. But, Sambo managed to keep his composure as he heard Diablo tell him, "I got the driver who took you on that bumper cart ride. Send the team up to Grant Park to play em' at baseball. Tell em' to bring their bats and gloves."

Now as Diablo anxiously waited, lusting for blood and action, he put a plan of diversion in motion. Sambo with one of his guys, approached a group of Italian women and began to flirt with them using explicit language, while grabbing on them aggressively. A few Italian men ran up in their face demanding they leave their women alone, while all the attention was on the men standing off, Diablo snuck up on one of their known top ranking men and snapped his neck. The rest of the Italian men then began to bust shots as Sambo and his men returned fire. From the other end of the park you could see Herby running on the front line, leading a crew of E.S.B. mob go-getters, all with guns in hand, who immediately engaged in a big shoot out at

Grant Park. Herby first two shots took out two of their men. One of the Italians then shot him in the arm and stomach, but his body was to numb from the drugs to even feel it. His eyes next locked unto the Italian he'd seen in his rearview mirror hanging out the truck shooting at him that day. He instantly squeezed the trigger of his gun in the man's direction as he chased him down with two other Italians. As the men ran and jumped inside one of their cars to escape, Herby came gunning, shooting all three men in the car, unloading his gun until it just clicked. When he ran out of bullets one half dead Italian rose up shooting him two times in the stomach before finally falling back to his death. The two shots knocked Herby down on the sidewalk but he bounced back up like a ball once he heard the sounds of sirens. He then took off running in the middle of traffic trying to flee while holding his nine Beretta in one hand and with his other hand his stomach where he took the gunshot wounds. All of a sudden, Sambo with two of his guys, pulled up beside Herby in a car they just stole to escape, yelling, "Herby, come on, Hurry up and get in."

Once he jumped inside the back seat, Sambo who was driving, asked him, "Herby you alright?"

He responded, "Naw, them bitches shot me in the stomach." Sambo next asked, "is that the only gun you got?" He replied, "Yeah, I just unloaded the clip on they ass. I need some more shells." One of Sambo's guys who was sitting in the back seat with Herby then snatched the gun from out his hand and began to hit him in the face with it until he passed out. As they all laughed at Herby being knocked out the man hit him once more waking him up. That's when Herby woke up fighting, engaging in a tussel with the man. As Herby fought for his life in the back seat, in a fight he was winning, Sambo pulled into an alley where they all jumped out shooting Herby to death while he was still in the backseat. After they unloaded their guns on him making sure he was dead they fled and later told Diablo they seen the Italians kill him.

***

Federal Agent Shabazz with a squad of uniform and plain clothes officers raided the downtown adult Ladies and Gentlemen's club, armed with an arrest warrant naming Teno for the murder of Mike Myer with pending federal charges. A manager and stripper at the club name Ti-Qila-D-Eata, who was there setting up for a party later, told him Teno wasn't there, hasn't been in weeks, and that she would call him when she does. Once Agent Shabazz seen Teno wasn't at the club he asked her, "Was he here the night them men came in here shooting?" She responded, "No, not to my knowledge. Sir. I don't believe so."

He then asked, "Where are the video surveillance tapes for that day?" She replied, "Sorry but they wasn't working that day." After her response he just looked at Ti-Qila-D-Eata for a moment directly in her eyes observing her nervousness as he told his officers, "Alright fellas, let's go."

Agent Shabazz next searched for Teno's unknown place of residency. Teno moved his mother Gloria to her dream home in Miami, after he came-up to keep her safe from his mayhem coming back to haunt him. The Chicago house he lived in was in his mother's name and documented as being vacant for rent by E.S.B. Realtors. This left Agent Shabazz frustrated hoping his place of residency was at one of his baby momma's house.

As Teno sat reclined in his Lexus coup driving down 87th Street real slow, Sheila was leaning over the seat sucking on his dick, with a Little Wayne song, "I wish I could fuck every girl in the world... playing out the speakers. He looked down one of his baby momma's blocks and seen the Feds rushing in.

Out of panic he hit the gas then slammed the breaks causing Sheila to slam her head on the steering wheel and dashboard, busting her lip. When she got to fussing, he pushed her out of his car, into the street, threw her purse out the window, and sped around the block. He parked and sat a block away observing the Feds raid and shake Lala's house down while she stood outside putting on a tantrum, cussing the Feds out. When they didn't find a trace of Teno they all jumped back into their cars rushing to Shaunika's house, his other baby momma who lived a few blocks away. Teno again parked a block away observing the Feds raid Shaunika's house with her coming out in a robe with some guy in his boxer shorts. As Teno said to himself, "Trifling bitch got my shorty around some nigga." he witnessed the Feds hand her a card. She then balled the card up and threw it in his face, grabbing her male friend by his hand storming back into her house. After that Teno did the only thing he could think of, call Big Face.

Later when Teno met back up with Big Face, Fats, and Diablo, Fats said, "All day them Alphabet boys been running in people houses, but for some reason besides the club they ain't fuck with none of us. I know they know we fuck with you." Big Face then said, "Yeah, we all got to be careful. Them bitches got their radars on us. Much as I hate to say it I think we all next, so we got to outsmart em' and come from under this shit.

But right now, Diablo you get Teno his new identity. Fake I.D., credit card the whole nine. Set him up a secure underground line. I'ma put our lawyers on top of it, but I'ma use your cousin Erika to do that." Diablo then said, "I gone put the goons on the streets to kill everybody who we think telling or even know too much. I got them F.B.I. boys myself." Teno then stated, "It's whatever with me. I don't give a fuck. I just want to murk all them Italian bastards before my glory ends. You feel me?" Teno was now officially on the run from the Feds.

***

In Ford City Mall's parking lot, two people got out a dark grey conversion Van, who looked like they played in a Tyler Perry and Martin Lawrence Big Momma movie. As they walked towards the front main entrance one of them smacked the other one on the ass cheek and said, "Diablo you got to switch that ass more. It's all in the hips baby." Diablo who was dressed as a fat nun to cover the tattoos on his face, looked at Teno who was also dressed like a Big momma character said slowly in a angry tone, "I done killed niggas for less. Don't ever do that shit again." They then pushed the glass doors open and proceeded through the hall towards the escalator. When two female shoppers seen them one said, "I'm glad my grandma don't look like that." The other one stated, "Yeah, they re pretty ugly aren't they? I feel sorry for their grandkids. Thank God for nursing homes, huh?" Soon as the two dressed like Big momma's stepped onto the escalator a five year old girl who was being held in her mother's arms pointed at them as she cried, "Run Mommy....Grandmommy turned into a monster."

The mother embarrassingly said, "Hush honey... I'm sorry Ma'ams, please forgive my daughter."

They just looked away giving no response. When they got off the escalator, they headed to a nearby Jewelry store. Once in the jewelry store, a female clerk behind the counter asked, "How may I help you ladies today?" She then looked into their faces and froze from the terror she seen in their eyes.

Teno pulled out an assault weapon from under his dress spraying rapid shots at two Italian men behind the counter, while Diablo jumped over the counter running into a back room where he released rapid shots at two more Italian men.

As glass shattered everywhere from Teno's rapid shots inside the store, the showroom windows shattered from an Italian man in the hall shooting at him. When Teno ducked the shots, Diablo came from out the back busting shots at the Italian man shooting the remainder of the showroom windows out. The Italian man took two o£ Diablo shots to the chest and fell to the ground, however, lucky for him, he was wearing a vest. He then quickly got up to run, with Teno and Diablo now chasing him down through Ford city Mall, while the female clerk was still standing behind the counter frozen but unharmed.

The Mall's security surveillance cameras showed two Big Mommas heavily armed with assault weapons chasing and shooting at an Italian man who pushed and shoved shoppers around in his desperate attempt to escape his pursuers. Armed officers moved in to secure and protect as frighten shoppers hysterically ran through the mall. Every time the Big Mommas seen they had an open shot without harming innocent shoppers, they took it.

The Italian managed to bob and weave every time until he fell over a baby stroller. Just as the lady pulled the baby stroller away the Big

Mommas ran up spraying his body with bullets at close range. Suddenly Diablo felt and heard bullets whistle past his ears. When he turned around witnessing three officers shooting at him, he squeezed the trigger of his chopper chopping all three officers' bodies up with a hail of bullets. They then tried to run toward the front entrance from which they came, but changed directions once they saw a group of officers coming from that way. As they ran through the chaotic mall shooting back and forth with officers they decided to run through a T.J. Max store that had an exit to the malls north parking lot. Once they made it outside to the parking lot, they ran up on a guy in a customized Chrysler 300 M with big shinny rims, who was parked up front showing off his car while he hollered at a female. They then snatched him up out the car throwing him to the ground and peeling out to make their escape.

As the man got up off the ground the woman snatched her phone number back from out his hand and said, "You won t be needing this since you don't have a car to pick me up in no more," He responded back, "Oh, it's like that, you car booty ass bitch! Fuck you then!" She then stated, "If you still had a car you could fuck me."

***

One of the E.S.B. main breadwinning drug trap houses was on 64th and Green. During the summer this spot raked in $350,000 a night from heroin, ecstasy pills, cush weed, and a corner whore house with the finest, thickest, young bitches you ever seen selling the best pussy, ass, and head you ever had. All this was on one block but what brought the most money and traffic was them triple stack ecstasy pills with the devil stamped on them that sold for twenty-five dollars. They were some serious hitters that had you rolling. Twenty-four hours a day, seven days a week, 64th and Green stayed packed like a never-ending block party. Law enforcement put cameras up on the block in an attempt to issue out secret indictments but the E.S.B. mob out-smarted them. They paid juveniles from five to ten years old to direct traffic and take customer orders while dealers ran up to serve customers with Halloween mask on to avoid being identified by the cameras. After some hand to hand exchanges some dealers would look up to the camera, give it a middle finger then run off in a cutway. Chicago's Big Brother surveillance cameras didn't stop a damn thing. It was like a live reality show of a Chicago block with drugs, gangs, whores, and murders.

During an average 64th and Green business as usual busy day, a black Suburban truck pulled up to make a buy. After a dirty little snotty-nose six-year-old boy asked them, Ya'll straight?" the driver asked, "Can I get ten jabs for this $80?

The little boy responded, "This ain't Jew-Town. Now pull up to the blue house and park."

When a dealer wearing a ski mask ran up to the truck and seen a truck full of men now wearing ski mask like him, he yelled, "On this truck!"

But, it was too late, the passenger doors of the truck flew open with two men jumping out on each side shooting up the block with assault weapons that had 100 round drums. At the same time this was happening two additional Suburbans blocked off each corner of Green street with men wearing ski mask jumping out chasing people to gun them down. All you heard was the sounds of automatic weapons, cries, screams, and yells. While all you seen was people scrambling in all directions, ducking behind cars, and people being pushed while bullets took them down.

Once the masked men empty their 100 round drums and burned out in their trucks toward Halsted Ave, they left 118 people dead with 73 more people wounded. They even left six dogs and two cats dead. This was known as the Green Street Massacre.

All the signs told that this was for sure a retaliation hit by the Italians for killing some of their men and one of their bosses in the Ford City Mall hit.

After the Green Street Massacre the E.S.B. paid for a number of funerals to be held at Gatlings Funeral Home on 101st and Halsted Ave, with twelve victims at a time to be honored in side by side caskets in ten funerals with the last having ten. Each and every funeral was jammed-packed for blocks. At this particular one all you seen in front of the funeral house was people hanging around the limousines, Cadillacs, and their best cars like a car show but instead these were mourners who used alcohol and weed smoke to cope with their loses.

Once inside the packed funeral home you witnessed twelve caskets with people in a line viewing their bodies giving their last respects. All you heard was cries from babies and grown people, until a woman jumped on top one of the caskets yelling, "Oh God, they took my boo, please take me with him." She then got inside the casket saying, "Baby move over, I'm coming with you."

All of the sudden the attention was taken off her when a man next to her viewing a body started shooting inside a casket at a dead body. He then flipped the casket over along with the one the lady was in.

Two of his accomplices in the back next pulled out hand guns to shot up the funeral, but they dared not take a shot when they witnessed a majority of the mourners was armed and now shoving guns in their faces as they disarmed them.

While a crowd of mourners up front stomped their man, they began to stomp and beat all three of them to death inside the funeral home. While this was going on inside, outside a drive-by shooting was taking place killing six people in front of the funeral home. But, before the drive-by shooters could make it up the block, some mourners who was hanging around their cars under the influence of drugs and alcohol that prayed for an opportunity of vengeance for their dead, upped their guns and recklessly ran into the street shooting up the Chevy they were in until it crashed into a parked car where they ran up to it shooting until all the men inside were dead.

This was a war between the Italians and the E.S.B. mob that had no safe zones.

***

One early morning four days after the funeral incident, two black Suzuki 1100 motorcycles rode side-by-side, Big Face on one and Fats on the other, both being hugged tightly by their passengers, the sexy but vicious Pocahontas twins. They all rode with black helmets, black Harley Davison jump suits and back packs, as they went up to 120 M.P.H. to make it to their destination on time.

For two weeks straight, at 6:48 A.M., the traffic light at 95th and Harlem would turn red with a blue Bugatti stopping in front, a grey Maserati in the middle, and a black McLaren last, all occupied by

Italian bosses. Today, as the light turned red with all three cars stopping in a line, two motorcycles, one behind the other, pulled up in the left lane beside them.

Once at a complete stop, the driver of the first bike grabbed an uzi out his backpack, and began to shoot inside the Bugatti.

The driver of the second bike also grabbed an uzi out his backpack but began shooting inside the black McLaren.

The female passengers jumped off the bikes locking and loading uzis as they ran up to the grey Maserati in the middle that they shot up.

Once the light turned green, the ladies jumped back on the bikes. The first bike popped a wheelie as they sped away leaving a bloody mess of three Italians dead and slumped over in their own blood.

After the Italians lost three of their elder bosses in that traffic light hit, they traded in their vehicles so no one would be familiar with their automobiles. They decided to send out some hitters to gun up every well known E.S.B. members cars.

One evening, around 3:30 P.M., a well known member name Booby gave his baby momma D.D. the keys to his apple red Chevy Broham to pick the kids up from school. He stayed home getting his money ready to recoup some drugs to sell.

On her way back with the kids, the hitters the Italians sent out spotted Booby's Chevy riding eastbound on 95th and Jeffery so they quickly rode up beside it shooting over 100 rounds before they realized it wasn't Booby inside. Then they rode off leaving Booby's baby momma, D.D, and his two eight-year-old twins, K.K, and T.T, shot up and dead inside his car as it sat in the middle of traffic.

***

One of the hitters from the Italian mob name Hector loved tricking off on a stripper name Kitten-Purr every weekend. But this weekend Kitten-Purr had different plans for Hector, as she sat in her living room grieving her husband's death who was murdered in the Green Street Massacre.

Kitten-Purr wasn't all that good looking in the face but her thick body made up for her gruesome face. Some guys use to call her Kitten-Poop as an inside joke for how her face looked. But, her big juicy titties, wide hips, big round butt, and thick thighs made you forget about her face and drove men crazy for her 40-26-56 figure. She was your average Chicago stripper whore who everyone took turns fucking on the low-low. Every club she danced at, men came in flocks to see her strip, trying to out-bid the next man so he could trick off with her after work. She was married and in love with her husband Mark.

One night, after Mark seen her strip, he couldn't help but to trick off with her and he was sprung ever since. He married her hoping to have her all to himself. He knew she was a whore but thought he could change her into a housewife. They were deeply in love with each other. She continued to strip and whore, but tricks meant nothing to her, her heart was with Mark.

Now when Kitten-Purr found out Hector was one of the shooters in the Green Street Massacre who killed her husband she eagerly got in contact with Diablo. She told Diablo everything she knew about Hector down to his freakish fetishes. How he liked for her to wear a strap-on to fuck him, piss on him, blind fold him, spank him, and a bunch of other weird stuff.

She was fully willing to do whatever Diablo told her to get vengeance for her one and only true love Mark.

In a Marriott Hotel room, Hector and Kitten-Purr tooted some lines of cocaine before she performed her usual routine with him. She first made him lick the sole of her nine inch high heels, then eat her pussy before she pissed in his face.

She next slapped him around and spanked him with a paddle on his ass until he begged for her to put on a strap-on to fuck him. Once she blindfolded and handcuffed him to the bed, she unlocked the Hotel room door. She then put a thirty-two inch strap-on dildo on. Now, possessed by that vengeance demon, she rammed the dry thirty-two inch strap-on up Hector's ass with no lubrication as she angrily told him, "You punk bitch faggot muthafucka you... Naw, naw, bitch don't scream and cry now. You weird, gay-fagget bitch you... I want you to feel all this pain you muthafucka you."

The door of the hotel room opened and Diablo and two of his guys came in. They tried to sit and wait for her to get it all off her chest so she'd get closure, but they couldn't take witnessing this freakish torture, so one of the men pulled her off him and told her, "Let us finish him for you. Now, please take that off and get dressed."

They cut Hector like a surgeon from chest to stomach. When they dumped his body in the Jacuzzi for his guts to fall out, Kitten-Purr ran over to his body, spit on it and said, "That's for my boo Mark you fucking freak. Now burn in hell you trick ass bitch."

***

While Sambo drove reclined in his black on black Escalade, smoking on some cush weed with his right hand man Pook and two of Chi-Towns finest trophy broads reclined on their sides, his "Birdman fire flame spitters" ring tone rang.

When he answered he heard, "All you E.S&B. niggas walking dead men. Oh, by the way, that baby picture of you in your mother's living room on the glass coffee table next to the lamp and Bible, is real cute. Also, I think your mother just fallen and can't get up. Ahhha ha ha ha."

When the caller hung up, Sambo hit the brakes, looked at the broads with a killer face and said, "Get the fuck out now."

As Pook watched the two scared broads jump out of the truck in the middle of traffic he asked, "What's going on fam?"

Sambo hit the switch to the stash box and told Pook, "Them bitches got my moms, fam."

When the dashboard opened up, Pook grabbed a 30-30 and a 40 cal that were stashed in it and began lock and loading them as Sambo raced to his mom's house with watery eyes and a face expressing murder.

Once he pulled in front of her house, Pook passed him the 30-30 while he jumped out with the 40 cal running to her front door that was already open. Once inside, Sambo seen his mom's body laying dead on the living room floor. He fell to his knees, grabbing her up off the ground, hugging her while he still held the 30, rocking back and forth crying, "Not my moms... Why my moms... Why not me instead?" As tears ran down his face he kissed his mother on the cheek and said, "I love you mom."

He looked up at Pook and said in a crying voice, "They took my moms, fam. I'm about to show these bitches a gangster for real now. I'm making their moms, grandmoms, even their little babies pay for this. After I kill their babies, I'm gone drink the blood then kill them. Ain't no mercy for nobody... You hear me?

After Pook called Diablo and told him the news about Sambo's mother, Big Face, Fats, Teno, and Diablo all came together with Sambo and Pook to get the big pay back. Most of the Italians moved their families to gated communities figuring they were all safe and out of harm's way. But that will never stop the E.S.B. mob.

On a Monday morning around 10:30 A.M., a gate security man was checking the list to see if Peoples Gas Company was scheduled to come in until he remembered Mrs. Lazureno called the front office earlier to inform him they were coming. He opened the gate allowing them to enter the gated community where they pulled into the Lazureno's family driveway. Sambo, who was dressed in a Peoples Gas hat and uniform, rang the door bell as he held an odd electronic device that made a buzzing sound.

When an old lady answered the door and asked, "How may I help you Sir?"

He said, "Hi, I'm Mr. Smith from the Peoples gas company. Is this the Lazureno residence?"

She answered, "Yes this is."

He replied, "Our office is reading some complications in your gas pipes, may we come in to check it out?

When she replied, "Sure", he signaled for the rest of the men to come in.

He said, "Mrs. Lazureno, I need you to get everyone in the house to come have a seat in the living room right away because my meter is detecting dangerous levels of carbon dioxide. My men need to come in with their machinery to fix this problem."

Four minute later, the entire Lazureno family sat in the living room. Mrs. Lazureno, who was 68-years-old, sat in a recliner, her daughter-in-law, Carla, a 44-year-old, sat on the wrap around couch. Carla's daughter, Zeda, a 21-year-old mother held her one-year-old daughter in her arms and sat on the couch with her mother. Carla also had a 14-year-old son name Tony who was now in the living room grabbing the remote to the big TV.

Once the other five men were inside the house with their large duffel bags, they put on ski mask and grabbed weapons out their bags. One of the men held a camera phone up to record the following events that was now to take place. With the Lazureno family faces of horror being captured on the camera phone, one of the men with a Mosburg pump shot the 68-year-old woman in the face, knocking her whole face off while her body still sat in the recliner.

As the other men restrained Tony and his mother Carla on the floor, one of the masked service men grabbed Zeda while another grabbed her baby and escorted them to the bathroom where she was forced to watch one of the men drown her baby in the tub all while another man recorded the incident.

One of the men then pushed Zeda down to her knees while he shoved the barrel of a 40 cal in her mouth. As she cried and mumbled with the barrel in her mouth, he pulled the trigger splattering her brains and blood all over the bathrooms vanity mirror.

The cameraman ran back into the living room to record Carla being beaten to death with a sledge hammer and her son Tony get stretched out on the living room table where one of the men slammed an ax down on his neck detaching his head from his body to be next placed on the side coffee table.

The men then took the family cat and dog out their cages. They put a leash on the little Chi-hua-hua dog and hung it to death on a ceiling fan. The cat they drench in lighter-fluid and set it ablaze. The men all fell to the ground laughing when they seen the burning cat run around the house bumping into walls screaming until it just fell and died.

Before leaving out one of the men told the cameraman, "Hey record this." He then poured a bottle of bleach in a large fish tank and said, "We leave nothing moving."

Now, as security opened the front gate to let the Peoples Gas truck leave the community, Mr. Lazureno received a message on his phone showing his whole family being heinously murdered. As he watched with a frighten look on his face, he fell dead from a heart attack.

Days Later

Diablo received a call from one of his sources who owned a Star Bucks coffee and donut shop downtown stating, "Dig homie, that Fed

Shabazz who working to take Teno and the whole squad down, just walked in ordering a large Cappuccino and a half dozen jelly donuts, but you ain't hear that shit from me. You feel me?" After Diablo responded, "Good looking." he hung up with a big smile on his face looking at Teno who was sitting beside him in the passenger seat of the conversion Van.

Once they pulled up to the Star Bucks, they saw Little Ray Ray and Baby 'D' hanging in front of the shop playing around with three fast little girls, so they made the little girls leave and put them on security before they posted up at the stores door. Now with Baby 'D' around back and Little Ray Ray up front, Diablo and Teno posted up on each side of the store's door waiting on Agent Shabazz to come out. Just as Agent Shabazz came walking out through the doorway with two other Feds, a police squad car pulled up in front of the shop.

Just then Little Ray Ray casually walked up to the driver side of the squad car to give the officer five quick head shots. Agent Shabazz with the two other Feds instantly drew their pistols, but pointed them in the wrong direction. That's when Diablo and Teno shots took them by surprise, killing one Fed instantly. When they seen one of their fellow agents fall to his death, they took off running to the back of the shop to escape the ambush, but Diablo and Teno gave chase. Once around back they squeezed their triggers to let the bullets give chase to the two Feds.

As their bullets took one down, they assumed he was dead and ran past him in chase of their main target, Agent Shabazz. That's when Baby 'D' seen the other Fed laying on the ground trying to call for back-up, so he ran up on him and asked, "Hey officer, you need some help? Need me to radio in for you?" As he stood over the Fed he pulled out a 40 cal, pointed it at the Feds head and said, "I already know the code. It's officer down."

As the Fed looked up at him saying, "No. Don't do it. Please." he shot him in the face several times.

Diablo and Teno then came running up to Baby 'D' angrily shouting, "That bitch got away. Fuck." While they stood their cussing expressing how angry they were Agent Shabazz escaped, a squad car came swerving around back real fast with Little Ray Ray driving. He yelled, "Get in before the 5.0 come!"

When they all jumped inside he said, "Look I came up. I got his badge and police gun."

Teno yelled, "Just get us the fuck up outta here!" When he hit the sirens and burned out, Diablo stated, "You little crazy bastard, cut that fucking siren off! Now get us a few blocks away and park so we can bail the fuck out and set this bitch aflame!"

Later that night as Teno and Diablo snuck in the back door of Erika's house, entering into the kitchen, they were confronted by Fats who just looked at them shaking his head side-to-side and Big Face who stared at them with a mean mug expressing disappointment and anger. Then Big Face said in a slow, angry tone, "What the fuck was ya'll smoking? Cause that shit had to have been the stupidest shit ya'll could of ever did. And what the fuck is wrong with you Teno? You don't fucking know you a wanted man? Because evidently you don't and you so fucking stupid you don't realize you just made your situation along with ours worse... Nigga we just came from nothing to a whole fucking lot real fucking fast, but we still doing dumb shit. We out here murking niggas ourselves when we got soldiers lusting to put in work to get a name with us. We fucking made it, but we too fucking hands on. We're literally wiping our ass with money, but look at us, we at war with them god damn Italians and now we got the fucking Feds on our ass. Thanks to this cop-killing spree we just graduated to the Feds top most wanted list. This all because we not using our fucking heads and money... How long ya'll think this shit gone last? What the fuck is we suppose to do now? Where in the fuck do we go from here? Do you know Mr. Devil... Satan... Diablo... or whoever the fuck your psycho, schizophrenia ass think you is. What about you Teno?... Cause you changed after them Feds ran in you rat ass baby mommas houses. Nigga I know you. Now you snapped out into this killer. You must think this shit a movie. This real fucking life nigga. Niggas out here dying and going to fucking jail forever!"

He was suddenly interrupted by yells from Erika screaming from out the living room, "Aye ya'll, They showing that shit again on the news." When the men rushed into the living room a flat screen TV showed the W.G.N. 9:00 P.M. News with it's top story about a shooting at Star Bucks downtown that left one cop and two federal agents dead along with one agent suffering from a gunshot wound. As the newscaster reported the story in details showing the scene with a picture of Teno posted up, Big Face just stared at him with a face of disappointment as he shook his head from side to a side.

W.G.N. news has been posting up Teno's picture and making coverage of the shooting all day. Agent Shabazz was on a personal manhunt for Teno which is why he recognized him as one of the gunmen at the coffee and donut shop. When he escaped the deadly shoot-out and checked himself into a hospital because of the gunshot he received, he gave reporters Teno's picture to post up with a number for anyone who knew anything about the gunmen who took officers lives and almost his.

Narrator, Lucifer

From my hood to your hood slanging, banging, murdering, and fucking. This how wartime is in the streets of Chicago, baby. Ain't no love hoe, love is nonexistent. See where I'm from it's no sunshine and the grass don't grow. 9.1 is the murder code and everybody got bodies. You murk or get murked.

Don't fake it cause them goons will come to lift your skirt. Yeah the Devils playing chess with all ya'll. You just a pawn in this self-destructive plot to murk and make all ya'll fall.

But, how about them E.S.B. boys? They got some serious beef with them Italian don't they? Innocent lives being lost and ruined. See war equals death and death equals more souls for me to collect. Is war the solution? Cause as the old saying goes, you live by the sword you die by the sword.

Now your boy Lucifer gotta go so I'ma holla at you later. But if you need me before then, just look in the mirror and say, "Mo bloody murder" six times, and watch me appear, Deuces!

Chapter 11

After the police shooting Teno had no choice but to lay low, especially with wanted posters being posted up everywhere of him. The original plan was for Teno to leave Chicago and hide out in Atlanta. The E.S.B. knew the Feds were expecting him to flee the city, and that they would put most of their man power and focus on the borders.What confirmed their assumption was the lack of manpower for his manhunt in the city. They had posters up but no arrest or doors were being kicked in.

Meanwhile, Teno went into hiding with a half black and Brazilian woman name Cherrilyn, whom he had an on and off relationship with for several years. He stayed laid cooped up in her north side loft while she ran all his errands. When she wasn't tending to his affairs she was laid up with him fucking all day, every day. Her 36-24-46 figure brought the sexual beast out of him. Their sexual intercourse usually kicked off with him licking her face like a wild animal before aggressively tearing her clothes off. Once they got to fucking in an animalistic manner they would engage in rough sex by biting on each other while growling until they both came. There were times when Teno would get horny by plunging a double stack ecstasy pill directly in her anus and another one in her vagina. She would then wrap her legs around his head for him to sloppily eat her pussy out and then blow and lick on her ass hole until she came in his mouth.

In Teno's mind, she was his soul mate. He was in love with her so much he asked her to marry him at a time when she could only say yes. That time was when she sat on his face in the sixty-nine position, moaning saying yes to his question while they both came at the same time. Teno wanted so badly for her to have his baby, so every day and night, he would pin her down to fuck the shit out of her in an attempt to get her pregnant. The day they found out, she was two weeks pregnant, they decided to sneak out the house for a movie and dinner at Dave and Buster's to celebrate the baby on the way as well as their engagement.

During this rendezvous, Teno remained unnoticed while disguised in a fake beard and wig. That was until a jealous ex-girlfriend noticed him hugged up with Cherrilyn walking out of Dave and Buster's. The jealous ex-girlfriend next grabbed her cell phone inquiring about the reward for Teno's whereabouts.

As Cherrilyn tried to pull out the parking lot with Teno laying across the back seat of her black Jaguar, a number of marked and unmarked squad cars surrounded them. Once all the officers and agents were posted up with guns drawn, Agent Shabazz who was still bandaged up from his wound held a bullhorn in his hand as he yelled, "Teno it's over son! Just get out the car slowly with your hands up and no one will get hurt." When Cherrilyn began screaming, "God no! This can't be happening. No!"

Teno jumped upfront and grabbed a Glock 40 out the stash box. Cherrilyn, with tears running down her face, looked at Teno and said, "Baby please don't do nothing stupid. Think about our baby and us. Please baby, don't do what I think you're about to do."

With his right hand he tightly squeezed the handle of his Glock, as he wiped her tears away with the other. He then kissed her passionately before telling her, "Stop crying. Don't worry about it. It's gon be alright baby. I ain't about to do nothing stupid. You know I love you right?"

She replied, "Yeah I know. I love you too Teno."

He then looked up and saw some news trucks filming the incident. He next got out the car with his hands up in the air yet still holding his gun. As he stood there looking at all them officers pointing their guns at him, everything got to moving in slow motion. After he heard, "Drop... Your... Weapon... Now!" something snapped out in his mind causing him to make his Glock explode seven shots toward officers as he rushed them in an insane attempt to escape, but the officers shot him down instantly.

Cherrilyn ran to grab Teno's bloody body as she cried out, "You motherfuckers better not have killed him. Baby, wake up. Teno, please tell me you're not dead."

Surprisingly, Teno began to spit up blood.

When she began kissing him all over his bloody face, officers pulled her up off of him, hand cuffed him to a gurney, and shoved him into an ambulance.

Back at 67th and Eberhart, Erika called Big Face to tell him "You ain't gone believe this, but dumb ass back on the news. He just got himself shot up and arrested by the police."

He replied, "You bullshitting. How did that happen?"

She replied back, "His silly ass went out to Dave and Buster's with a Ho bitch and got caught in the parking lot."

He next stated, "Erika, say it ain't so."

She replied, "Oh yeah, it's so. The news just said he gone survive but he's in federal custody facing a gang of charges."

Later that night, Teno's lawyer came by Erika's house to inform her of all Teno's charges. Furthermore, he had no bond, and the key witnesses against him are Little 'O' and Tom Tom. But that wasn't all, he also told her his arrest was just the beginning of the entire E.S.B. mob take down. They had a total of forty warrants out for Big Face, Fats, Diablo, the Pocahontas twins. Little Ray Ray, Baby 'D', and other E.S.B. members. The only name that the lawyer didn't say was Kareem's which she knew was only because he had been away at college. Everyone else was facing every charge in the book from murder, attempt murder, kidnapping, drug trafficking, manufacturing, distribution, and much more. They were even hitting the E.S.B. with the Rico act and classified them as a terrorist group against the United States.

Once Erika was done talking to Teno's lawyer she was so relieved that her and her girls names wasn't on that indictment list that she prayed out loud, "Lord, I promise I'ma get my shit together starting right fucking now. I thank you that my name wasn't on that list, Amen!"

After Erika informed Big Face of all the indictments, he instructed the E.S.B. mob to lay low. But first, they were to make sure that anyone who memory knew too much got their minds erased with lead erasers. Now with a majority of the E.S.B. top ranking men on the run and unable to move around, Kareem had to start running back and forth from school to the city to run the organization. He was focused on making sure they held their grip on the city. However over all he was trying to help his brothers come from under this drama, while continuing to stay out the drama. Kareem was in charge and he knew he had to make a difference so he agreed to meet with Don Cappino from the Italian mob.

After Don Lazureno's death, the last Don surviving from their war was Don Cappino, and he quickly waved the white flag to end the war. This war started from a debt the Italian mob placed on the E.S.B. mob in accusing them of killing Mann and robbing her for some drugs and money that belonged to them. In exchange for peace and no further retaliation, the Italians agreed to squash the debt and surrender one of the three areas that they still had a strong hold over to the E.S.B. mob. This was with an understanding that they would allow them to fully operate out of their two remaining areas with no intervening from the E.S.B. mob period. None of the other E.S.B. bosses favored Kareem's decision, but they all honored it because their plates were full with drama.

Now with the E.S.B. mob knowing Tom Tom and Little 'O' had been working with the Feds and that they were the reason all their names was on that indictment list, every member plotted to behead the two Judas's. Tom Tom and Little 'O' had no idea the word on the streets was they were telling. They knew Teno was in custody but was ignorant to the fact that he has a constitutional right to confront and know who his accusers are.

On a rainy Chicago night, Big Face and Fats sat in a gangway smoking on some cush weed under the moon, as they tried to figure out how and the hell did they get to this point, and a plan to get out of it. Suddenly Big Face eyes locked unto an all white Escalade that rode and stopped at 88th and Saginaw directly in front of Shelia's house. His blood shot eyes then looked at Fats as he asked, "what kind of rims do that hoe ass nigga Little 'O' got?" Fats replied, "Some sixes." Big Face said, "This nigga just pulled up in front of that dick sucking rat bitch Sheila's house." Suddenly, the only thing revealed in the mist of the night-was the white from Fats eyes widening and teeth from a grin. They then locked and loaded their weapons and sprung into action with one coming from one side of the street while another came from the other side. As Fats came from the alley, hopping a gate into Shelia's backyard, Tom Tom who was taking a piss beside her house looked up at Fats and took off running towards the truck, however, the shots from Fats sawed off shotgun made his head explode causing his body to drop on the sidewalk. Next Big Face with perfect timing came from the other side of the street steaming his muffler with the air holes on a tech nine with an extended clip. He gave Little 'O', who was in the driver's seat continuous bullets to his face until he ran up to the Escalade finishing the job, leaving what was left of Little 'O's face pressed against the horn.

Early the next day news reporters went around with law-enforcement to broadcast live coverage for the world to see some raids and apprehensions of forty top E.S.B. bosses, Lieutenants, Generals, and members. Officials had several squad cars all over the city raiding the mob at the same time to a avoid members giving others a heads up warning. Officials caught some of them sleeping, so they drug them out in their robes and slippers, yet a few of them wasn't going out without a fight.

As the raids took place, one E.S.B. General named Pook seen the cops and Feds surrounding his home. He then instantly sent his wife and two kids running out the front door with their hands up while he ran into his armory that was in his bedroom closet.

As officers ran in through the front and back doors, proceeding up the stairways to the second floor, Pook threw a smoke bomb from the top of the staircase and shot off a street sweeper killing five officers before he chased the rest out of his home.

After the officers retreated, Pook busted his living room windows out, flipped over his leather couch, and began firing rounds at the officers encamped around their cars in front of his home.

As officers returned fire, he threw a grenade out the window blowing up a squad car. After the explosion, they exchanged heavy fire back and forth for about three minutes until shots from Pook ceased. That's when officers began to march back in until the front porch blew up with just the top step to the door left. But, that didn't stop them from marching forward.

Once back inside the house one of the officers tripped over a line that caused another explosion in the living room that took four officers lives. As officers proceeded ahead with cautions up to the second floor, Pook ran into a back room to jump out a second floor window. He hit the ground and jumped back up like a ball busting a Tommy gun this time at officers surrounding the backyard before he hopped the neighbor's gate making an escape.

A C.P.D. helicopter received a dispatch, "Be on the look-out for a six foot black male, who is armed and dangerous. He's shirtless, wearing a pair of black basketball shorts and a pair of red and black Jordan gym shoes. He's been spotted running eastbound on 79th and Eastend. We need a chopper to locate him."

Within twenty seconds, a C.P.D. and W.G.N. news chopper had live surveillance on him running through an alley, hopping a gate into a yard where officers now had him surrounded. After an officer announced, "You got ten seconds to drop your weapon." he took a deep breath, twisted his fingers to throw up the E.S.B. sign, squeezed the trigger, and went out in a blaze of glory shooting at officers as they shot him down to his death.

The whole incident was shown live on W.G.N news, C.N.N. news and many other news channels.

The day ended with thirty-five E.S.B. members apprehended out of the forty raids. A few members exchanged fire with law enforcement but later surrendered with no casualties. The only raid not shown on the news was when officers kicked in freaky Toot's door to find him butt naked having a ménage à trois with two women and lines of cocaine everywhere. It was like he knew they was coming because when they came in the room with guns drawn he kept fucking and said, "Just let me bust this last nutt right quick, then I'm all yours. I just gotta get my Charlie Sheen on first."

Out of shock, the officers just watched him toot a line of cocaine, take a swig from a bottle of Hennessy, and bust his last nutt over the two women faces before they handcuffed and took him into custody. They drug him out with his dick hanging and cocaine still on his nose as he yelled, "I been had my money right and ready to go. Now, go tell my two bitches to go wash their faces so they can come visit me in division nine A.B.O. Now let's hurry so I can make it there in time for commissary. I need my Zoozoos and Wamwams. E.S.B. or die bitch. I'm an E.S.B. soldier, I thought I told ya!" He next twisted his fingers in the cuffs to throw up the E.S.B. sign as officers shoved him in the police car naked, where he began to throw up all over the back seat.

***

Kareem knew Joe-Joe was due in court to testify tomorrow against Kevo, therefore he had to be hiding in the city somewhere. He sent Diablo out to find him before he got a chance to speak a word on the witness stand.

In the meantime, Kareem got a call from Big Face to meet him and Fats at a safe house in the Jeffery Manor maze where they kept a majority of their drugs and money. Once Kareem entered through the front door, all he saw was money machines counting money while garbage bags of money sat around with guns and drugs everywhere. The radio played a Young Jeezy song, "Counted so much paper it a hurt your hands."

Once Fats looked up and seen Kareem he said, "We got some good fucking news to tell you homie."

Kareem replied, "Naw nigga, I got some good fucking news to tell ya'll. But I wanta hear ya'lls first."

Big Face looked at him with a smile on his face as he announced, "It's official little brother, we putting all this shit behind us, we're retiring. We about to split these mills three ways and go hide out in Mexico. Somewhere out in the mountains where Santana got his own Militia running shit. So ain't no bounty hunters like Dogg coming to get us unless they want their heads mailed back in a fucking box." Fats next stated, "We told Santana and the Nigerians we was done, they both said they were glad we finally came to that decision." Kareem asked, "So where this Mexico shit come from? Big Face explained, "Santana gone have his people get us up out the states. He waiting for Kevo to get a bond so he can send him with us. He say he want you to finish your school thing then come with us. He spoke highly of you, how you too smart for this shit anyway. How you turned our dirty money clean. He say just keep all that shit in your name so we can live like kings off it in Mexico. But yeah little brother you made us into real businessmen. We just fucked it all up by not washing our hands in time." Big Face eyes got watery as he fought to hold his tears back as he stated, "We fucked up Kareem. Them bitches trying to give Teno the death penalty and we got to leave him behind. That's our fucking brother. It wasn't suppose to end like this. I'll rather stay broke flipping eight balls and 63's if I knew it was gonna end like this. This wasn't worth all the blood and loses."

Fats then passed Big Face a blunt as he told Kareem, "That's our good fucking news now what's your?"

Kareem stated, Don't trip fam. We gone be good. I'm projected as a N.B.A. first round draft pick. They been talking about me all day on E.S.P.N. saying I'm the hottest thing from Chicago since Derrick Rose. So, we set fam. We just gotta get ya'll up out of here and find a way to help Teno. There's always a way."

Big Face then stared at him with a proud face as he entered a state of peace no longer feeling like his life was vain, but that his purpose was complete by helping Kareem make a dream a reality. The men then gave Kareem a hug as they patted him on the back and excitedly told him how proud they were of him. After the hugging session they all went back to work packaging up the money to take with them, until Kareem asked, "Is ya'll gonna take the pussy and the kids with ya'll or what?"

Fats answered, "Hell yeah, I just hate this dude gone bring my nagging-ass big sister with him."

Big Face Stated, "I'm bringing my son too but I wish Keshia would let me bring his mother Renae cause she got the bomb on the head, no homo but she be sucking the sheets up my ass."

The men then all broke out into a laughing frenzy.

As the sun began to set, Diablo pulled up in the driveway blowing the horn. Once they all came outside, he popped the trunk of the Chrysler 300 revealing Joe-Joe lying hogtied inside. When they all looked at each other in shook Diablo said, "This his car so we can burn this bitch up if ya'll want to." Fats then quickly snatched the duck tape off Joe-Joe's mouth to shove the barrel of a black nine millimeter down his throat.

Big Face yelled, "Naw nigga, what you doing?"You want the neighbors to call the police? Kareem go get them hunting knives off the table." Soon as Kareem stepped inside the house a flood of marked and unmarked squad cars with a news Van rushed the block.

Agent Shabazz knew Kevo and the E.S.B, were linked together so he figured they would be the ones who try to stop Joe-Joe from testifying. So, from this hunch he decided to place a tracking device on Joe-Joe the moment he arrived in the city. Now when the agents assigned to watch over Joe-Joe reported Diablo was just spotted kidnapping him, they were instructed to stand down. Agent Shabazz theory that Diablo would lead them to Big Face and Fats proved right when they spotted all three of them in the driveway.

Once Big Face seen the cops and Feds raiding, he told Fats, "What you waiting on, hurry up and kill that bitch."

Fats, still holding the barrel in Joe-Joe's mouth, let off four shots before running into the house behind them.

Once inside the house, they all put on bullet proof vests and strapped up with army guns, backs packs full of ammunition, and grenades. Big Face then told Kareem, "You grab all the bags of money. We gone fire them bitches up so you can hop the gate to Crack head Willie's yard a couple blocks away. We got a Brougham Chevy in his garage." He threw him the keys to the Chevy and said, "We need you to take this money to Erika's house. That's where we gone all met back up at later. We need you to take our shorties and B.M's over there too, so we can leave from there."

After they all locked and loaded their weapons, Fats, with a serious look on his face said, "It's E.S.B. or die now. I love ya'll. Big Face, if I don't make it, you better take good care of my sister and niece."

Diablo cut in with, "Nigga, your punk ass better make it up out of this. You gotta take care of my sister and her shorty or I'ma kill your ass again. You think I'ma let you fuck my sister and die? You better be more scared of me than them and take your punk ass out there in murda mode."

When the mix C.D. in the stereo began playing Little Wayne's Carter Two, "Hit em up, Hit em' up..." They instantly got into kill mode, running out the house kamikaze style, throwing grenades, shooting a Street Sweeper, an A.K., and a Tommy gun.

When law enforcement seen three crazy nuts rushing them throwing grenades and releasing fire, it caught them off guard, forcing them to quickly retreat. Once the E.S.B. chased them off the block, they took the squad cars the officers abandoned to block off the streets entrance.

Now that the sun had set leaving this Jeffery Manor block lit by the moon, a C.P.D. helicopter along with a W.G.N. news chopper, flew over the block to give live coverage and also a visual with a spot light. The news showed Diablo on one end of the block shooting a Tommy gun with a 100 round drum at officers, while Big Face was on the other end shooting an A.K. wildly, and Fats in the middle of the block shooting a Street Sweeper at officers who were trying to enter the block by sneaking in between houses.

Kareem, still unnoticed, was knelt beside a garbage can gripping a 40 Cal with a backpack full of money on him. Suddenly, Kareem heard Fats screaming Big Face's name as he ran towards his end of the block. He just felt Big Face was in distress so he took off running to help his brother. By the time he made it to his end of the block where they had a police car blocking off the street, he saw the bodies of five officers laying dead and Fats knelt down holding Big Face who was losing a lot of blood from a gunshot he received to his right leg.

Kareem ripped a shirt off one of the dead officers to wrap around Big Face's leg to stop the bleeding.

Fats noticed a few officers trying to move in so he quickly

reloaded and went back to getting it in, shooting every officer dead in sight.

Kareem told Big Face, "Come on, I'ma drag you up outta here."

Big Face looked at him and said, "Naw little homie, just go into my backpack and get me a few of them grenades out and reload me, cause you must don't see me bleeding under this vest."

Fats came back holding his chest as he said, "Them bitches got some Teflon bullets, fam. But I ain't dead yet and these hoes gotta come with me."

Big Face looked at Kareem and said, "Get your ass the fuck up outta of here now nigga! You know our motto is E.S.B. or die! It's die with us, but you, you E.S.B. you got to represent us and our struggle. You got a chance at life. A chance to leave this hell. This all we got. We living in hell. We alive but we been dead a long time now. Look around, how many niggas you know make it up out the hood? Almost none and you one of the blessed ones. Now, when you make the last winning shot in the N.B.A. flicking your wrist, remember to represent us by throwing up that E.S.B. sign." He looked at Fats and said, "You ready to blaze this bitch up?"

When he responded, "You know it." Big Face took his E.S.B. chain off, handed it to Kareem, and commanded, "Now you get your ass the fuck up outta of here!" Kareem then gave them hugs and a kiss on their foreheads. Once he run off, Fats said, "Kareem!"

Once he turned around, he seen Fats holding his E.S.B. chain up as he yelled, "What you ain't gone take mine to remember me?"

After he grabbed the chain and ran off into the cutway, disappearing between two houses, all he heard was them igniting grenades and releasing none stop shots.

Kareem, covered with Big Face and Fats blood, finally made it unnoticed to crack head Willie's garage where he started up the blue Chevy Broham on chrome twenty-six inch rims. As he drove off, he turned on the six T.V.s to watch the incident live on the news. Just when he turned on 95th and Stony Island Ave, to get on the freeway, the news showed Diablo getting shot in the ass. Diablo was then shot in both legs as he fell to the ground dropping his weapon feets away. As he crawled to retrieve it, officers rushed in to take him into custody.

Moments later, the News showed Big Face and Fats last stand.

Tears ran down his face as the screen showed a war scene that looked like it came out of an army movie that killed Big Face and Fats, plus many officers instead of actors. He cut the T.V's off, gripped the wood grain steering wheel tightly and drove straight to N.I.U. with blood all over his clothes, a 40 Cal on his lap, and a Louis Vuitton back pack on the passenger seat with millions of dollars in it.

Alicine Payne a W.G.N. news castor reported, "The last two top bosses of the E.S.B. mob were killed during a shootout with Federal agents and officers today who were trying to execute warrants for their arrest. The Mob's Chief of Security who was also involved in the shootout was finally shot and taken into custody. This shooting took the lives of sixteen officers and left nine wounded. Once law enforcement gained control of the area they searched a resident believed to belong to the E.S.B., and found a record number of heroin, cocaine, marijuana, lean, and ecstasy pills. They also found 2.2 million in cash still in money machines. Law enforcement took down thirty-eight out of the forty warrants issued, leaving two members still at large. The E.S.B. was a well-known notorious, murderous, drug-dealing mob that controlled ninety percent of the Midwest drug trade. They made Chicago its base for its pipeline. The streets of Chicago will now be safe and drug free with this take down. This is the day that Chicago received its streets back. Now to our weather with Tom."

Narrator, Lucifer

Bad boy, bad boy, what you gone do when they come for you? Them E.S.B. boys showed us, didn't they? But hey, it ain't over yet. If they don't fuck around and resurrect like Jesus,

I still got plenty of souls waiting to fill their shoes, to continue my mayhem. I control many souls even yours. As you read this, I'm reading your soul, controlling your thoughts and emotions. Now let's see how this shit ends in this and in your life. Aaaahahaha..haa...ha...ha. It's that dude the soul survivor Lucifer G. signing out yet again fool!

Chapter 12

In the locker room before the start of a fourth quarter basketball game Kareem accepted a collect call from Teno and heard, "Shalom Ahk, you know I was just checking you out on the screen. Aye man, you out there like a straight bomb. Get your head into the game homie!"

Kareem stated, "How can I when the Lawyer I got for you just told me you threw a chair at him, then fired him? The man say he can get you life instead of the death penalty. What's wrong with you, you wanta die?"

Teno replied, "I'm at peace with God. I'm no longer being deceived by Satan, My spirit with Yahweh so it's gone live on. I gave Satan and these people one life and they can have it cause I got a new one that they can't take from me, you feel me?" Kareem replied, "I see you went to jail and got real deep into this Hebrew Israelite thing. I been trying to get you to convert to Islam for the longest but I'm just glad you at peace homie. You know I'm blessed all praises due to Allah. I just miss my brothers." Teno replied, "You suppose to be representing and living life for us especially after all we sacrificed for you. The way you playing ain't representing us homie. Now get it in for all of us."I love you homie now stay up."

Before they hung up Kareem stated, "I got ya'll fam. Much love bro,"

At the start of the fourth quarter, Kareem hit the court with his mojo back. He brought his team from being ten points down to a tie game with only seconds left on the clock. He caught the ball from a pass and attempted to make a three point jump shot. As he flicked his wrist releasing the ball from his hand he twisted his fingers to throw up the E.S.B. sign. As he held his hands in the air representing E.S.B, the ball went through the net making a swoosh sound. The shot gave the Chicago Bulls a win at home over the Los Angeles Lakers. Kevo from a United Center courtside seat jumped up yelling, "Get them rings baby! You the man, Kareem!" While his teammates held him in the air he yelled, "That was for Big Face, Fats andTeno!"

Kevo was released from federal custody when the only witness against him got murdered. Upon his release he announced his retirement from the drug game to partner up with Kareem and Santana on some major business investments. He is now a respected businessman who resides in a 5.5 million dollar home in Miami, Florida with his wife Brandy.

Teno got the death penalty by lethal injection on July 4, 2010. This was after the Illinois Governor Rod Blagojevich refused to take his 2.4 million dollar pay off for a pardon. Sources reveal he only refused the bribe because he got word the feds were pursuing charges against him for selling a State Senate seat. This pardon of a Chicago mob boss would raise too many eyebrows. If it wasn't for that the political game of pay to play would have paid off for both parties.

Once Erika finished cosmetology school, she opened her first beauty salon on 79th and Ashland. After Big Face's death, she stop hustling. She now owns five beauty salons and is currently married with twins on the way.

Nicole is a successful choreographer, teaching famous rhythm and blue singers dance moves. She also runs a dance school in L.A, where she lives with her daughter. Once a month she flies to Chicago with her daughter to faithfully visit her husband Iky in Stateville C.C.

Tammy stayed in the drug game until she went broke from continuously being robbed. She left Erika's house to move in with one of her boyfriends who got her hooked on drugs. Her mother got custody of her daughter Cece due to her drug problem. She started bouncing from one hustler to the next, fucking and sucking on whoever would buy her something to keep her up with the material world and living the high life. She soon became H.I.V. positive. The day she found out, she committed suicide by cutting her wrist.

Diablo went back to Stateville C.C. with four natural life sentences for six police murders and over twenty E.S.B. mob related murders. He reclaimed his crown over his kingdom by stabbing two inmates to death who got some drugs in without giving him a cut. He laid law down that everything that goes on, must go on through him and nothing without him.

Sambo was one of the thirty-five caught in the mob raids. When law enforcement kicked in his door he exchanged fire with them. He eventually surrendered once he realized he had no way to escape.

Little Ray Ray and Baby 'D' were both at their girlfriend's house when their mother's doors got kicked in during the raids. They fled the city once they realized only five of them remained free before Big

Face, Fats, and Diablo got took down.

They're now responsible for going down south from one state to another robbing and brutally killing big time drug dealers. They're on the feds most wanted list as 'Chicago's baby 9.1 bandits. Every major hustler piss in their pants at just the thought of them two being in their town. The two were last seen in Atlanta at a club called Magic City. They robbed, shot-up, and shot a local drug dealer in the face while he got a lap dance at the club.

The sexy Pocahontas twins were captured in the raids. They now reside at Dwight Women's Correctional Center. They both have natural life sentences for drug conspiracy and a number of E.S.B. mob related murders. This includes a traffic light hit they did on motorcycles that was caught by traffic cameras. They now control and terrorize the women's facility.

One day in their cell, the twins had a young dike girl eating their pussy out, when one of the twins got mad the girl stopped licking before she came. One of the twins held the girl down while the other one shoved a broom stick handle inside her pussy and broke it in half. With the other half of the stick they took turns beating the girl until she was a bloody mess.

Once Jamarion got ran off the block by Big Face he realized the street's wasn't for him. He took Big Face's threats serious plus the choking he received hurt. But, he later realized he was only looking out for his best interest which is why he put a few thousand dollars in his pockets. He stayed out the streets and focused on school, to later attend Grambling University. After graduating, he got a job working for the Coke Cola company as the Eastern Regional President. He now gives thanks to Big Face for running him off to a better life.

The streets got real dry with the E.S.B. gone. This opened it back up for the Italians to reclaim their territory, in which they grasped with ease.

The money Kareem ran out the safe house with that day, was the money he used to put in bank accounts for all of Fats, Big Face's, and Teno's children. He set up college funds and personal money they would get once they turned twenty-one. He also signed over the Chrysler dealership to Big Face's baby momma Keshia, the club over to Teno's baby momma Cherrilyn, and the real estate company to Fats baby momma Gelisa since they were always loyal to his brothers.

Big Face son Corey by Renae, Fats son, Deshaun by Gelisa, and Teno's son, Aaron by Cherrilyn became close establishing bonds like their fathers had. Years later when they were all around the age of thirteen they went into a game room where the owner, an old Mexican man, just stared at them and said, "You guys don't know me but your fathers Big Face, Fats, and Teno were like sons to me. So, that means you all are like my grandsons. And if you all are like my grandsons that mean I got to take care of you all like I did your fathers. Here look at these pictures of me with your fathers in our glory days. Oh by the way, you guys can just call me grandpa Santana."

To many people the E.S.B. mob now rest in peace. But their spirits continue to live on in these treacherous eastside streets of Chicago. Especially through their sons who eyes now glow fully possessed with that inherited spirit of their fathers.

On the eastside of Chicago, the Muslims had their Holy day and service on Friday, the Hebrew Israelites had theirs on Saturday, and the Christians on Sunday with the same tune coming from off their lips speaking, "Our people are miss-educated, lost, and blindly running to their own destruction, destroying everything in our path. None of us want our kids to repeat the sinful lives we lived. How can a people destroy a community that their children are left to live in? Look around, we're leaving our children to inherit destruction. They're also repeating the cycle making it worse for the next generations. Do you want your children to grow up playing in your old mess or shall I say Doodoo?

Once the W.G.N. news was done broadcasting its top story about another Chicago student being killed in front of Carver High school, a black woman in her eastside apartment pressed the remote to turn her TV off, then faced the east as she prayed, "Baruc atah Yahwah, grant mercy and bless our children. When will our people see the truth, no longer repeat this cycle of destruction, and return to you? May the war between good and evil prevail with the establishment of your kingdom. Selah."

***

Condolences goes out to the children of Chicago who lost their lives to violence. Saving our children starts with you, act now.

In Memorial: to all the school kids who lost their lives to Chicago's violence.

Condolences goes out to the young man, Derrion Albert, a 16 year old honor roll student who on September 24, 2009, was murdered while walking home from Fenger High school, on the south side of

Chicago, Illinois, by several other young men.

Derrion is just one example of Chicago teen violence with too many more names who we have not forgotten. We must become aware and act on saving all our children from this violence. The victims to this violence is our children who are losing their lives, our children who are mentally lost committing these crimes, who are ruining their lives, and our future generations which are our children's children. Please help! It starts with you acting now.

ABOUT THE AUTHOR

East Side or Die (Chronicles). The reality of sex, money, gangs, and Chicago's murder rate is exposed through these childhood brotherly bonded boys who formed the East Side Brothers (E.S.B) mob and took over Chicago's drug market with help from a Nigerian and Mexican Cartel. The E.S.B rose from the bottom making the eastside of Chicago a major pipe-line for the mid-west region. You get to enter a Chicagoans world and witness how their everyday lives are in living that Chi- Town street life. As with the Eastside Brothers at an early age most go to jail and die in the game with one making it to actually do something with his life.
This poetic Chi-Town urban novel is dedicated to our beloved children who lost their lives to Chicago's violence.

It's an overall story view of what that life's like, that's destroying us and being passed down to our children's generations to repeat its destruction of our generations. It's Chi-Town or nothing. East Side or Die Chronicles!

Past, Present, Future, (People of Color transition to true knowledge). A intellectual black heritage book full of history, documented facts, soulful poems, informative topics covering people of color issues, how it all relate to people of color, and more. From ancient past to the future, it's filled with true knowledge and wisdom on many subjects we all need to be knowledgeable of as a group of strenuous people to be reckoning, progressing into a prosperous future.

Coming Soon

Look out for the C.T.G brand, shops and more books by Christopher B.Trotter. ChristopherTrotter11@GMail.Com.

Books coming soon by Christopher B. Trotter

East Side or Die Chronicles 2, Generational Spirit of Gangsta's.

Past, Present, Future; the Volumes. Each chapter from the original book broken down in volumes with more details, documents, facts, poems, and more.

Past, Present, Future; Poetic spoken words. A book with just all the soulful poems from the book and more.

A recommendation; To kiss the soul of a woman, by Martice Hanible. A book filled with heartfelt poems.

www.ingramcontent.com/pod-product-compliance
Lightning Source LLC
Chambersburg PA
CBHW060327260626
47160CB00007B/2708